Quiz

Fluffy, your next-door neighbor's cat, tells you he saw a murder, a human murder. What do you do?

- A. Call the police (right, as if *they're* going to believe you).

- B. Tiptoe through the Redwoods and look for the body by yourself (are you crazy?).

- C. Ask Tanner Rutland, ever so nicely, to help you, since Fluffy is *his* daughter's cat (and if that doesn't work, seduce him).

Your next-door neighbor claims your cat saw a murder. What do you do?

- A. Run for the hills. (Lili Goodweather can't actually talk to animals. Can she?)

- B. Make sure Lili stays away from your daughter (you don't want the woman's nonsense infecting Erika's young mind).

- C. Follow wherever Lili leads.

If you picked A or B, you've obviously lost your sense of magic and need to lighten up.

But if you picked C, then you're about to step into another dimension, Lili Goodweather's dimension, and there's no doubt, it must be magic.

Other sexy, scintillating titles by

Jennifer Skully

Sheer Dynamite
Drop Dead Gorgeous
Fool's Gold
Sex and the Serial Killer

Jennifer Skully

IT MUST BE
MAGIC

HQN™

ISBN-13: 978-0-373-77197-4
ISBN-10:   0-373-77197-5

IT MUST BE MAGIC

www.HQNBooks.com

Printed in U.S.A.

To John Surette

You will always live in our memories

As will your motto

Can do, will do, doo-doo, John!

ACKNOWLEDGMENTS

Linda Simi, for the hours spent probing my brain and pulling out the magic, and Cathy Maxwell, for giving wings to the idea. Jean Cummings, always a lifesaver, always there with a well-taken point and encouraging word.

My agent, Lucienne Diver, and my editor, Ann Leslie Tuttle.

IT MUST BE
MAGIC

CHAPTER ONE

"CAN YOU REALLY talk to animals?"

Translation: "I don't believe you can. I also don't believe in ghosts, vampires or Bigfoot. And let's not even get into the Santa Claus myth."

Lili Goodweather was used to skepticism from adults, but not in twelve-year-old girls. Children had a wonderful capacity for believing in the unbelievable. Unless it got squashed out of them early on. Which was obvious in Erika Rutland's case.

A shivering tabby sheltered in her arms, the girl stood on Lili's back stoop, her grandfather a step behind her like a guardian angel. Erika's straight blond hair straggled over her shoulders and dark circles beneath her blue eyes contrasted with the pink glow of childhood innocence on her cheeks. Sign of a type A personality, poor kid.

Lili decided to save the metaphysical explanation of how she communicated with animals for later. "Yes, I can."

"Well, since you *say* you can, then will you try talking to Fluffy?" Erika cuddled the animal in her arms.

The cat's dilated pupils almost obscured the sunflower-yellow irises of his eyes, and the tremors coursing his back made the hair stand on end, giving him a fluffier than normal coat. A muddy blue aura like a churning river shrouded his body.

"Of course I will." Lili pushed open the screen door, letting in the warmth of the April afternoon.

Roscoe Rutland—Rascally Roscoe as Wanetta had called him—stuck out a steady hand and pumped Lili's with a firm grip. "We're happy you're living next door to us."

She'd officially moved into Wanetta Crump's house five days ago, but she'd met Erika and her grandfather during her many visits here when the elderly lady had been alive.

Roscoe had plenty of lines on his face, but they were happy lines, as if he laughed a lot and had thoroughly enjoyed his many years, which Lili guessed to be about sixty-five. He also seemed a bit on the thin side, as if he ate to live instead of living to eat.

With a sparkle in his blue eyes, he added, "And my son Tanner can't wait to meet you."

Lili had never met Erika's dad, the mysterious Tanner Rutland. All right, he wasn't really that mysterious, not like an ax murderer or anything, he just worked a lot and didn't seem to be home much. Lili had her doubts Tanner Rutland had professed any interest in meeting her. People often said exactly the opposite of what they meant out of politeness, and Roscoe's glowing statement sounded a little fishy.

Lili's long skirt swished across her knees and the tops of her boots as she backed up against the open screen door. "Welcome to my home." Saying that felt grand.

Stepping inside, Roscoe's gaze dropped to the checkerboard floor, which was once again black and white instead of gray…and gray. "You've done a great job with the place."

"Thank you." Wanetta's house had been built in the early 1900s, with a wide front veranda, a swing hanging from the porch rafters, shutters and dormer windows in a tiny third-floor attic. The upstairs bathroom had a claw-foot tub, and of the three bedrooms, Lili had taken one for an office. The living room fireplace would be wonderful for rainy winter nights, but the kitchen, even with its ancient appliances, was Lili's favorite spot. She often sat at Wanetta's big wood table in front of the window to watch the blue jays squawk at each other and dig for worms. The forest was almost in her backyard.

She'd spent the week cleaning from top to bottom, and was thankfully done, since tomorrow, Friday, she had to get back to work at the flower shop.

"Wanetta was grateful for the way you came running whenever one of her cats needed help. Not to mention the litter box problem." Roscoe plugged his nose dramatically.

"That was easy enough," Lili answered. Wanetta had left Lili with seven cats. This week, they'd gotten discombobulated with her move-in. Taking to hidey-holes throughout the small house, they had yet to come out, except at dinnertime or to slip through the laundry room cat door for a potty break. When Wanetta had first called on her in distress—she'd had a full house of twenty at the time—Lili had talked the cats into using the universal outdoor facilities instead of the indoor carpeting. The house was as fresh as a daisy now, after Wanetta had had the carpets torn out and discovered the hardwood underneath.

"I'm so glad she left you the house," Roscoe went on.

"I can never thank her enough for that." Lili was terribly grateful for the lady's legacy to her. On her salary at the flower shop, Lili could never have bought a house, even in the little town of Benton, which was nestled in the mountain foothills an hour and a half south of San Francisco. The town was twenty minutes by bus from the beach (and the Boardwalk amusement park, which Lili loved) and the deep forest was only a ten-minute walk outside the back door. As much as she missed her parents after their retirement move to Florida, she couldn't bring herself to leave her hometown. There was no more wonderful place on earth.

"Grandpa, do you think we could talk about Fluffy now?"

Lili understood how Erika felt. Adults, they talked, talked, *talked,* when there were more important things to be done. Such as getting to the business at hand and helping Fluffy.

"Why don't we sit down?" They all crowded around her kitchen table, she in the middle, Roscoe to her left, Erika on her other side with Fluffy in her lap.

Before Lili could do a thing, Fluffy growled low in his throat, and his gaze shifted to kitchen floor central.

Einstein had slipped in on silent kitty-cat paws and was now sitting in the middle of the checkerboard floor, her tail swishing. A regal Russian Blue with soft, sleek, silver-tipped fur, she'd been with Lili for seven years, and she was generally a great help in interpreting animal issues.

Looking at Einstein, Fluffy's muddy-blue aura shifted, deepening, swirling. Lili wasn't sure if other people saw auras the same way she did; she only knew how an animal's aura made her *feel*. And Fluffy was mad as all get-out at Einstein.

Einstein merely flicked her tail in irritation.

"I don't think they like each other," Erika said as she rolled her fingers in Fluffy's coat. He settled, and his aura ceased swirling. Erika's touch obviously had a positive effect.

"Someone invaded somebody else's territory," Lili explained.

Einstein had been the invader when they'd first moved in, with an abrupt rebuke from Fluffy, and though Lili had hoped the two could get over the animosity, Fluffy wasn't backing down. Einstein claimed the marmalade male didn't like females who were more intelligent than he was.

The guy's a wimp. What self-respecting tomcat would answer to Fluffy?

Animals thought in pictures and most humans thought in words, but over time, Lili and Einstein had managed to translate their differing thought processes quickly. Lili received an image of a tomcat having his masculin-ity…er…Einstein could be very graphic in her imaging.

Have some sympathy, Lili admonished. People didn't realize that names were extremely important in the animal world. Names were images. Alpha dog. Protec-tor. Fluffy lost all his dominance every time Erika called him by the name she'd given him. Animals revealed their names if their owners knew how to listen, not that animals could actually be *owned,* per se, especially not cats. If anything, it was the other way round; a cat owned its human. That was certainly true for Einstein.

But explaining all that to Roscoe and Erika right now was ill-timed. "Let's discuss how I talk to animals."

"Yes, please." Erika regarded her with intense blue eyes. She had the serious gaze of an old person. Or a skeptic.

Lili flicked her long hair over her shoulders and clasped her hands in her lap. "Well, first I look at their colors." She touched Fluffy's marmalade fur. "Not the color of their coat, but the colors around their body." She cupped and circled her hands for effect. "Their mood is reflected in the colors encompassing them. Just like people."

"You mean an aura."

Lili beamed. "Yeah. An aura."

"It's supposed to be an electromagnetic field surrounding the body. But *I've* never seen one." Erika raised an almost white brow several shades lighter than her hair, and her meaning was clear. Since she'd never seen it, it probably didn't exist.

Skeptic she might be, but little Erika was a smart one. Where had she read about auras? "Not everyone can see them. You have to be…open."

"What's my aura look like?"

Well. Erika had a bit too much brown in her yellow aura, as if she were feeling stressed about school, or something. But Lili didn't want to tell her that. With a child, it could be counterproductive. "It's yellow. Which means you're creative, optimistic and easygoing."

Erika blinked. Once. "Okay."

Lili didn't think Erika was those things at all. But she had great potential if she could rid herself of the stress.

Finally, the little girl said, "How else do you communicate with animals?"

"Animals think in pictures. And I can see them. We sort of—" she tipped her head, thinking of the best way to describe how she communed "—send movies back and forth, like Netflix."

"Netflix are DVDs you send through the mail. I don't think that's how *you* do it." Obviously Erika was a literalist.

Roscoe made a sound a bit like a stifled snort.

"It's the best analogy I could come up with," Lili offered.

"It was a very nice try." Ah. Erika was a *polite* literalist. "May we please begin? I have homework to finish, and my dad will be upset if I'm not done with it by the time he gets home." The child was definitely a tough nut to crack.

"You might as well face it, Lili, Erika doesn't think you can do it."

She'd dealt with a lot of nonbelievers. It didn't bother her. Really. She was so not bothered by it. Most pet owners didn't care how you helped their animals, even if they figured it was nothing more than intuition and lots of probing questions, as long as their problems were solved. In the end, Lili figured out the meaning in the images she saw and unraveled the mystery. That was all that counted. "I promise to try my best, Erika."

"My dad says don't confuse efforts with results. It's all right to say you don't think you can help Fluffy."

Don't confuse efforts with results. Well, that was a rather cut-and-dried way of looking at things. What if a little girl studied as hard as she could and still got a C on her test? Didn't that mean the teacher, or the parent, needed to try again as much as the child did? Lili was starting to understand the dark circles beneath Erika's eyes. Performance anxiety.

Lili leaned forward and scratched Fluffy under the chin. The cat shivered. "Why don't you tell me what happened, why you think something's bothering him?"

Erika blinked. "Isn't that cheating? My dad says that's how palm readers do it. They study your body language and ask a bunch of questions before they even start reading your palm, then they use all the stuff they learn and make it sound like they actually read it in your hand. People are very gullible. And that's not magic."

"I never said what I did was magic. I just listen." Lili touched Erika's hand. "But there's lots of magic in the world. In things like the beauty of a sunrise or an early morning mist rising through the trees or the salty taste of the ocean on your tongue. Don't you believe in magic?"

"Those things aren't magic. They're nature."

The poor child. "Then I guess you don't believe in magic."

"My dad says magic—"

Lili cut her off. "I'm not asking what your dad thinks. What do *you* think?"

Behind her, Roscoe held his breath. Lili felt it in the very stillness of the kitchen air.

"Sunrises and mist in the trees and the ocean are there all the time, so there's nothing magical about them."

But every sunrise was different, and each time you strolled through the trees or scuffed your bare feet in the sand was unique. Erika Rutland couldn't see that.

Every child was born with the ability to see the magic in a sunrise, yet somehow, by the age of twelve, Erika Rutland had lost that ability. It was a tragedy. Maybe it was because she'd lost her mother when she was only two. Lili had learned that from Wanetta. "Why did you bring Fluffy if you didn't think I could help him?"

Erika glanced to her right. The answer was obvious.

"Your grandfather talked you into it."

"He said it couldn't hurt."

It wouldn't hurt, and Fluffy *would* get better, but Lili wasn't sure Erika would get over losing her ability to see magic.

"All right. Let's talk about the goal here," Lili said carefully. "We want to help Fluffy. So any information you give me can only make this quicker and easier."

Roscoe raised one white eyebrow. "Go ahead, honey." Then he winked at Lili.

Ah. Here was the believer in the family.

"He sleeps on the porch at night," Erika finally said, "but he wasn't there this morning when I got up to feed him. And he didn't come when I called. He wasn't even home by the time I had to leave for school."

"We heard the coyotes last night," Roscoe added.

Coyotes, while a natural part of life in the mountains, could be terrifying. Lili had heard them last night, too. They did hunt by day, but their howls carried farther in the stillness of the night. The sound of a pack zeroing in on the scent of some little animal was enough to send chills down the spine. The excitement of the chase, and worse, rang through their collective voices, an eerie, eager yipping and howling. Wanetta's cats slept inside.

"I thought Fluffy was a goner," Erika whispered. "He's *always* there in the morning for his crispies."

Cats had excellent internal clocks. If you didn't wake

up to give them what they wanted, they woke you up. Einstein would sit on Lili's pillow and stare at her until she opened her eyes.

"You must have been worried about him all day at school."

The girl's eyes misted, and her bottom lip trembled. It was the first sign of emotion she'd displayed. "I was," she whispered, then sniffed. "He was hiding under the front porch when I got home this afternoon."

"About an hour ago," Roscoe clarified.

"What was he like when you found him?"

Erika folded her body over the cat, hugging him against her abdomen. "He scuttles under the bed or behind the couch if I move too fast. And he hasn't stopped shivering."

Definitely some sort of trauma. Lili looked at Einstein. All the cat did was blink.

Lili would have to go in blind. "Let's get started."

She leaned into Fluffy and stared into his yellow eyes a long moment. His pupils adjusted even as she watched, her reflection shifting and morphing in his gaze. Staring at an animal could be a sign of aggression, but she'd discovered it also could be a form of hypnotism. Although who was being hypnotized, she was never quite sure. Finally she closed her own lids and found herself sitting in a tree with a long stretch of open meadow before it and the dense forest behind it. Well, she wasn't exactly sitting, but cowering high up off the ground on a branch, her body scrunched up against the trunk. She smelled wet grass, damp earth and the grape-jelly scent of a carpenter ant. An oak tree. Carpenter ants loved oak trees. The ants tasted good, too, like grape jelly, just as they smelled.

Dead leaves rustled off to the left of the tree. Lili trembled with Fluffy's terror. Something was out there. A human smell, yet rank, like raw meat left out in the sun. Light filtered through the trees, flashing off a gray object covering a human head, a helmet. And a sound, like the thud of a mallet into a wet, squishy sponge. The human wielded a tree branch or a stick, using it as a weapon. It rose and fell, rose and fell, repeating the horrible squishing sound each time it landed on…something. A misshapen thing on the ground.

Goose bumps peppered Lili's skin. Her heart raced as Fluffy's did. She wanted to run, but she didn't want the human to see her. All she could do was cower in her tree and hide.

Lili couldn't breathe, terror clogging her air passages and setting loose a drumbeat in her ears. She opened her eyes and dispelled the image. Einstein crouched in the middle of the checkerboard floor, her fur standing straight up along her spine. While Einstein couldn't see into Fluffy's mind, she could tag along on Lili's trip, catching glimpses of what Lili saw and definitely feeling the terror.

It was Fluffy that amazed Lili now. His colors swirled and lightened, then he blinked and started purring. It was the oddest thing, as if sharing the vision eased his burden.

Erika smiled and bent to nuzzle Fluffy. "He's purring."

Lili didn't catch a single sarcastic image from Einstein.

She couldn't tell Erika or her grandfather what she'd seen. What Fluffy had seen. Lili had to think first. Was it real? Had she misinterpreted?

Roscoe looked at her, the laugh lines on his face distorted into worry lines. "Are you all right?"

She was far from all right. Fluffy was far from all right despite his purring. But she couldn't tell Roscoe. "I'm fine. I always feel disoriented—" freaked out! "—after I do that."

Her hands were shaking, and she clasped them in her lap.

"Wanetta never said it took this much out of you."

It never had before. But then she'd never seen anything like this. She was used to dealing with nothing more severe than cat-box issues and dogs that snapped at their human's hand.

Lili smiled, and she forced it all the way into her eyes to make Roscoe feel better. "I'm fine. Really." Though *fine* was a word that could mean anything from "I'm okay but not great" to "I'm totally lying about how I feel."

She had to act normal. She had to come up with something to tell Erika and her grandfather that wouldn't worry them. At least until she figured out what to do. "Fluffy was hiding in a tree last night—" she gulped, searching for a lie "—while the coyotes were out. So he's a little wary right now. I think the best thing is for you to keep him inside at night until he calms down."

Fluffy hadn't seen coyotes running some poor animal to ground. Lili didn't think she'd misinterpreted anything.

Fluffy had witnessed a murder. A *human* murder.

CHAPTER TWO

"LILI TALKS TO ANIMALS, and she said we have to keep Fluffy inside until he's over the trauma of seeing the coyotes rip some little animal to shreds. Lili says there was lots of blood and gore." Erika shuddered, then peeked through her lashes to gauge Tanner's reaction.

Tanner ignored his daughter's dramatic description of Fluffy's trauma. He had a feeling it was greatly exaggerated to garner his sympathy, especially when he caught Roscoe's smile before he wiped it off his face. Instead Tanner thought of the couch he'd replaced last year because Fluffy had taken to marking it as tomcat territory. Not to mention the scratches at the bottom of every door in the house and the claw holes in the kitchen screen. Fluffy didn't like closed doors. The cat didn't like a lot of things and was the bane of Tanner's existence, but Erika adored the monster, though it was the furthest thing from a "Fluffy" that Tanner had ever seen. They should have named it Loki after the god of mischief in Norse mythology.

But Fluffy wasn't the important thing in Erika's tale. No, it was the lady named Lili. "So this woman claims to talk to animals? What, like Dr. Dolittle?"

They had a crackpot for a new neighbor. He should

have paid more attention to who was moving in next door. Wanetta had been sweet as all get-out, and Tanner missed her. She always had a big smile and a kind word, and she'd loved Erika like a granddaughter. But her cats had fertilized his entire backyard. He was forever stepping in their mess when he was able to find a few hours to work in the garden.

"Is that the Dr. Dolittle in that ancient movie from the sixties, or the newer version with Eddie Murphy?" Erika asked.

Tanner rolled his eyes. "You watch too much TV. Roscoe is going to have to cut down your allotment."

His father turned the volume down on the TV. And smiled.

He'd talk to Roscoe later about exactly what he allowed after school. "Did you get your homework done?"

"Yes, Dad. I did it right after we talked to Lili."

"And do you think it was all correct?"

His daughter gave him a superior smirk. "Of course. So, can we let Fluffy stay inside? I promise I'll put him out to go to the bathroom right before I go to bed, and I'll keep my bedroom door closed, and I'll let him outside as soon as I get up." She looked at him hopefully, big blue eyes misting up.

His daughter had him wrapped around her little finger.

"Let me talk to Fluffy." Not *talk* as the cat woman talked to animals, talk as in staring the tomcat down and letting it know who was boss. Tanner knew he was going to say yes to letting Fluffy stay in for the night, but he had to put on some kind of show.

"Don't yell at him, okay." Erika, the little scamp, blinked back patently phony tears and even let her lip quiver. "Lili says yelling damages his delicate psyche. And he's in a very bad way right now."

Lili. He'd have to talk to the woman about the nonsense he did *not* want his daughter's head filled with. "I never yell at Fluffy."

Roscoe cleared his throat. "Ah, yes, you do, Tanner."

Erika nodded vigorously. "You do, Dad."

He pulled the heavy tabby cat onto his lap, and it started purring. Which *was* a tad unusual, at least while sitting on Tanner's lap, but he took advantage of the cat's momentary lapse. "If I yell all the time, then why does Fluffy like me so much?"

Erika blinked. "He's got Stockholm syndrome."

Tanner gawked at her. "What?"

"Stockholm syndrome. You know, where the captive starts to identify with and feel sympathy for his or her captor."

"I know what it is." Then he laughed. Where did his daughter come up with these things? And with the straightest face. God bless. She was only twelve years old and so damn smart, he wanted to cry. How had he managed to raise someone so absolutely wonderful? "Fluffy does not have Stockholm syndrome."

"Lili says—"

"I don't care what Lili says." He was sure Lili *hadn't* said anything about Stockholm syndrome. Tanner tipped the cat onto the floor, slapped his hands on his knees and stood. "Tonight is fine. We'll talk about what to do tomorrow night…tomorrow. And right now, what's for dinner?"

Roscoe jumped to his feet. "Meat loaf and mashed potatoes."

"What about the vegetable?" It was important for a growing girl to get her vegetables. While Tanner could have picked up fast food on his way home from work, he didn't want Erika hooked on the stuff.

"Broccoli."

He hated broccoli. But it was good for Erika, so he'd force it down, too. "Go wash your hands, sweetheart."

Erika dashed out of the family room, Fluffy tucked under her arm like a bag of laundry.

As soon as she disappeared up the stairs, Tanner turned to Roscoe. "Tell me more about that woman in Wanetta's place."

"Lili Goodweather? She's pretty."

"I don't mean her physical characteristics. Did she supposedly talk to Wanetta's cats?"

"All the time."

Tanner combed a hand through his hair, then did a wind-up motion with his hand. "And? What else?"

"Wanetta left her the house in exchange for all her help."

Damn. "She bilked the old lady out of her house?" He definitely should have paid more attention to what was going on over at Wanetta's place.

"It wasn't like that. Wanetta thought of Lili like her own daughter. She wanted to help her. And she didn't want the pound to take her cats. She wanted Lili to take her time to find the perfect homes for them."

"Fine. So this Lili isn't a con artist. But taking Erika over there—"

"It did the child good. She was in a bad way when Fluffy didn't come home this morning. It broke my heart." Roscoe put a hand to his chest. "And when she did find him after school, it damn near broke my heart *again* watching her try to cheer him up without success." Roscoe gave him a glower. "So I'm not sorry I took her to Lili."

Tanner felt the usual stab of guilt that he wasn't there when Erika needed him. With each successive promotion, his home time was eaten away. He intended to be home by six o'clock, but three nights out of five, it was seven o'clock or later. Not to mention the weekend work he brought home with him.

"Now I have to get the meat loaf out of the oven."

Tanner halted him. "I'm glad you took her over there. I can see it helped her." Even if Tanner didn't approve, Roscoe's heart was in the right place.

His father smiled. "Lili is a nice girl, Tanner. You'd like her if you'd give her a chance. Go talk to her. See for yourself if she's a good or a bad influence." Then he hustled off to the kitchen.

"I will," Tanner murmured as he went upstairs to change out of his work slacks.

He hadn't always seen eye to eye with his dad, and he had a load of issues with the way Roscoe had lived his life, flitting from job to job while he'd tried to sell his musical compositions, which he'd never done despite his efforts. In many ways, Roscoe had abandoned Tanner's mom, left her for weeks on end while he pursued a dream that had never become a reality. Until she'd died in a hospital bed of cancer with only her nineteen-year-old son at her side. Roscoe hadn't made it home in time to be with her for the end.

Yeah, Tanner had issues with Roscoe, but his father had been a godsend since moving in five years ago. And Tanner forgave everything when compared to how

Roscoe loved and cared for Erika. Tanner worked over the hill in Silicon Valley, an hour-plus commute each way, and that was on a good day. But he'd wanted Erika to stay in the same house she'd been born in and have the semirural upbringing she got in the mountain foothills. With Roscoe, there was someone at the house when Erika got home from school so she wasn't a latchkey kid, or worse, hanging out at a mall. He shuddered to think about the four years before Roscoe had hit hard luck (not that he hadn't *always* had hard luck) and had come to live with them. For the first few years after Karen had died, Tanner had had to entrust his precious child to day care. He'd woken up many a night in a cold sweat worrying.

Roscoe had saved him from all that. He'd saved Erika.

So now Tanner had put aside the things for which he'd long resented his father. What he cared about was that Erika grew up well loved, with a good, practical head on her shoulders. She would go far in life. He chuckled. Stockholm syndrome. Only *his* daughter would come up with something like that. She was so perfect, he marveled again that she was his.

And that was why he'd be paying Miss Lili from next door a visit. He didn't want her infecting his daughter's sensible mind with a bunch of fanciful thinking.

ROSCOE PULLED THE MEAT LOAF out of the oven and stuck a knife in it. Ah, perfect.

Even more perfect was Tanner's upcoming after-dinner trip through the hedge. Sort of like Alice down the rabbit hole. Tanner wouldn't know what hit him. Roscoe wasn't sure if Lili could talk to animals, but he'd seen and heard some unexplainable things in his long life, and he was willing to give the girl the benefit of the doubt. Lili Goodweather wasn't traditional. She wasn't conventional. She wasn't prissy. She was sweet, caring and full of vim and vigor, the influence Erika needed.

Tanner was a good father, though he did have a tendency to work too hard and play too little, but there was one big thing Roscoe faulted him on in raising Erika. The poor kid had no dreams. She wanted to be a finance major when she got to college and planned to climb to the top of the big corporate ladder, like her dad, who was a big finance muckety-muck over in Silicon Valley. What kind of dream was that for a twelve-year-old, for God's sake? Not a *dream* at all. If her mother had lived, God bless her soul, she would have shown Erika the magic in the world. Karen had had the magic herself.

Lili was magic, too.

It wasn't as if Tanner hadn't had dreams once upon a time. Why, he remembered the kid talking about growing up to be a great anthropologist who discovered the missing link. But when Tanner had grown up, he'd thrown away his fancies, the good with the bad. Yet some dreams deserved to see the light of day. Roscoe knew; he'd striven toward his all his life. Even now, music played through his mind. He wanted that kind of dream for Erika. Something that made life worth living. Helping Erika do that had become Roscoe's new dream, replacing the old.

Sending Tanner over tonight was the first step in getting him to see how good Lili could be for Erika. And maybe she was what Tanner needed to get that stick out

of his butt. She could be more than good for the boy, if
he let himself live a little.

They *all* needed someone like Lili in their lives.

EINSTEIN HAD BEEN HANGING close the entire three hours
since Erika and Roscoe had left. During the first hour
after her "talk" with Fluffy, Lili had made herself three
cups of green tea with honey and a slice of lemon. Then
she'd started to think realistically. The horror hadn't
worn off; it had…receded.

She wasn't discounting the severity of it, but you had
to control a problem rather than let it control you. When
problems took over, they paralyzed the thinking process.

So Lili took control. She'd performed a million Google
searches for information on a body found in the local
mountains. Nada. Not even a missing person's report.

So what was she supposed to do? She certainly
couldn't call the sheriff's department and say, "A cat
told me there's a dead person within a mile of my house.
And the cat saw the murder!"

Wanetta's house was on the edge of town at the top
of a winding, paved lane that wasn't wide enough to
have a stripe painted down the middle. The neighbor-
ing homes backed onto the forest and meadow, and there
were numerous hard-packed dirt roads that led to ram-
shackle dwellings. Benton had its share of mountain
men, like Buddy Welch, who was rumored to be antiso-
cial. Lili had never even seen him. Their small town was
as close to country living as you could get in the San
Francisco Bay Area. Most people worked over the hill
in San Jose or Silicon Valley. Lili didn't know everyone,
and they didn't know her. She didn't have an "in" with

the county sheriff. She rode her bicycle to work; she'd never even been stopped for a speeding ticket. So *who* was she supposed to tell about what Fluffy had seen? Who would even believe her if she did tell?

Will you quit the pity party. Which amounted to Einstein flashing her an image of four women sitting around a table with tears streaming down their faces. A scene from *Desperate Housewives?* Einstein loved TV. Sometimes—most of the time—Lili doubted Einstein's claim that she was the reincarnation of the real Einstein. She could not imagine Professor Einstein being hooked on *Desperate Housewives.*

"I'm being realistic. I can't go to the police without something solid. What do we know right now?"

Nothing. What Lili got from the cat was the red circle with the line through it. Although for Einstein it was more black than red. Cats weren't color blind, but they saw more or less in dark and light. They also didn't have the same acuity as humans, especially up close, so Fluffy's images were a tad blurry.

"It was a man. I'm sure of that." With a branch or stick, something with a bulge on one end, a silver tip. Since Fluffy had been looking down, she couldn't distinguish the man's height, plus he stooped as he…used the stick. She couldn't make out his face, only the top of his head, which was covered by a helmet

"Do you think he was a biker?" It had been bowl-shaped like the helmets Harley riders wore. It was gray rather than black, though that could have been a trick of the forest lighting. Or a product of the ways in which cats saw differently than humans. Cats couldn't actually see in complete darkness, but their eyes let in a lot more available light. To her human eyes, Fluffy's images looked like daytime, but it could have been much later.

She stared at Einstein. The cat blinked her green eyes. "I should have asked Erika the last time she saw Fluffy before he disappeared. We'd get a better idea of what time it happened."

Duh. A dunce cap meant *duh.* Or *you idiot human.*

"You're not being very helpful."

That's because I'm near death's door. Feed me. Food bowls pranced across her mind's eye.

At least feeding the cats was something constructive. In the kitchen, Lili lined up the bowls and began opening cans. She'd tried feeding them in a rotation format, but everyone wanted to be fed first and she'd given up. With the first pop of a top, eight furry bodies started milling around her legs. Einstein stretched up to the counter and watched.

And Lili talked. "We have to get more out of Fluffy. I shouldn't have pulled out so fast." She'd let the shock take over. "How do I do it without telling Erika?"

Roscoe. Lili saw the possibilities in Einstein's image.

She set the first three bowls on the kitchen floor and the mob stormed them. Lili projected an image of order to the room at large, which didn't work at all. There was something about food and cats that defied order.

She smiled despite her inner turmoil. There was Einstein's silvery-blue coat, then white with black nose and black spots on white, calico and tortoiseshell, tiger-striped and leopard-spotted and Siamese elegance. Wanetta had always been taking in strays. She'd fattened them up and calmed them down, had them fixed, then had gone about locating good families to take them.

The knock on her back screen door had her whirling. A man stood in the shadow of her back stoop. She'd forgotten to turn on the outside light. Tall. Solid. Light-colored hair. That was about all she could tell. But Lili *knew*. Mysterious Tanner.

He was the answer to her prayers. She could tell *him* about Fluffy's vision. It was the correct thing to do, anyway. He was Erika's father.

The only problem was, with the state of her kitchen, eight cats in all, he was going to think she was a crazy cat lady. And after that, who knew if he'd listen to her.

"Don't rush right into telling him about Fluffy's sighting," she whispered to herself. "Just be yourself."

But if the *cats* made him think she was a crazy cat lady, being herself would make him run for the hills.

ROSCOE HAD UNDERSTATED. Lili Goodweather wasn't pretty; she was stunning, with dark hair flowing to her waist and a smile as brilliant as a summer day. Her silk tank top left her shapely shoulders bare, and her long gossamer skirt, which accentuated her willowy body, matched the color of her eyes, an odd, vivid shade the color of lilacs in full bloom. Wool socks brushed the hem of her skirt, and her footwear nullified the otherwise delicate nature of her clothing. The boots were some sort of weird fashion statement, but wasn't that only for adolescent girls? Lili Goodweather was closer to thirty, more or less.

"You must be Mysterious Tanner." She held the screen door open and smiled brightly.

"Mysterious Tanner?"

"I wondered if you really existed. Roscoe and Erika

talk about you, but I've never seen you. I thought maybe they made you up." She had the plumpest, sweetest-looking lips.

Dammit, he didn't want to be looking at or thinking about her lips. "I'd like to talk a minute."

She stepped back, handing the open door off to him so it didn't smack him in the face. Then he saw them. Wanetta's cats. She'd had only seven, yet it appeared a miniature herd of cattle grazed on the checkerboard floor. A writhing mass of bodies emitting a low hiss, like an ant army attacking picnic remains.

Then a sharper, louder hiss was followed by a growl.

"Serenity, behave yourself," Lili admonished.

In that heap of squirming felinity, he couldn't tell which one had hissed and which one had growled. Lili scooped up a dark, striped cat and a food bowl, then set them both down to the right of the main herd.

"Cats like irony," Lili said. "Serenity isn't serene at all. She doesn't like to share, not that cats ever *like* to share, and she's the first to pick a fight over nothing." She threw her hands palm up in the air and smiled. "What can ya do?"

One regal, gray cat stretched, swiped a tongue over its sharp little teeth and looked at him, an oddly assessing look. Then it hopped from the middle of the melee, jumped onto the kitchen table and sat. And stared. Its green eyes fixed on him with...well, he couldn't call it intelligence.

"Einstein, quit staring. It's rude."

The cat blinked and settled down onto its belly, tucking its forelegs one by one to its chest. And continued to stare.

"She thinks you're fascinating," Lili offered.

"She told you?"

"No. She's keeping her thoughts to herself right now."

There was his opening. "That's what I'd like to talk about."

"Einstein's thoughts?"

"No." Then he stopped and looked at the cat, its eyes trained on him like a laser beam. "Why do you call it Einstein?"

Lili glanced at the cat, then back at him. "She doesn't like to be called an *it*," she whispered, then raised her voice to a normal level. "She says she's the reincarnation of Einstein."

"*Says?*"

"Well, she didn't exactly *say*. But when we were discussing what she wanted to be named, she flashed me this image of Einstein—" she tipped her head "—and I knew what she meant."

"How did the cat know what the real Einstein looked like?"

Lili grinned. "That's it exactly! She couldn't have known. That was before she started watching TV. She says Einstein came back as a cat because cats are earth's highest life form."

Was she joshing him? Tanner couldn't tell. "Are you sure?"

She leaned in, her scent wafting over him, and murmured, "People and animals should be allowed their fantasies, don't you think? Between you and me, with her sophisticated, snarky attitude, I think she's got a lot more Joan Crawford in her."

This was exactly the sort of thing he didn't need Erika exposed to. "So, about why I came over—"

She beat him to the punch. "I'm glad you did, because I wanted to talk…" She trailed off, looked at him, quirked her mouth and started over. "About Erika. And your dad."

She tipped her head yet again, and her hair fell across her shoulder to caress her breast. Tanner lost his train of thought.

"Roscoe's such a doll," she went on. "You must be so happy that he's with Erika. My parents moved to Florida. It was warmer, and my mom wanted to be somewhere warm. Only she didn't like the dry heat in the desert." She glanced up, as if realizing she'd prattled on way too much. "Anyway, I miss them. So it's great that Erika has her grandpa with her." She stopped and looked at him. "I'm babbling, aren't I?"

He smiled but didn't contradict her.

"I don't usually babble—" Again she stopped. "I do babble, but I'm babbling more than normal. You make me nervous."

He made her *nervous? She* unbalanced *him.*

He didn't want to delve into the why of it. "Having Dad around has been great for Erika." He needed the conversation back on track. "Speaking of Erika, she's why I came over."

"She is so smart. She knew all about auras and psychic scams. She's very grown-up."

His daughter was his weak spot. He could talk about her all day, he was so damn proud. "She's got a good mind."

Lili let out a gasp he felt as well as heard. "She's the cutest little thing. So blond. And all those big blue eyes."

"All? She has more than two?"

She laughed, a seductive sound even worse—or

better—than the gasp. "You know what I mean. She's like a little Heidi. And she loves Fluffy. I've never seen a girl more devoted to her cat." She hugged herself and oohed.

The woman made him dizzy, the way her body moved, her exuberance about utterly everything. He didn't think she was capable of giving a straight yes or no answer or completing a thought in only one sentence.

He looked at the cats milling about the kitchen floor or licking now-empty food bowls as if there might be one missed micron. They licked paws or jaws or chests with swipes of long tongues. And he couldn't help thinking about…licking. And food. And Lili Goodweather. "Are you a vegetarian?"

She turned her head and looked at him out of the corner of her eye as if she couldn't figure out where that question came from. Neither could he. Food associations. He also had this odd desire to know more about her.

"You *talk* to animals," he clarified. "You don't eat them?"

"Oh no, I'm a total carnivore." She wiggled her shoulders, touchable, bare shoulders. "I mean, I don't eat a cow after I've talked to it, but I rarely talk to cows, anyway. I figure it's nature. You know, the predator and the prey. If Bigfoot decided to have me—" she put a hand right between her breasts, in case he didn't know who the *me* was she referred to "—for dinner, why, that's in the natural order of things."

Damn. He imagined having her for dinner. Or dessert. Or both. He'd been having blatantly erotic thoughts about her almost from the moment she'd let him in her door. Not that he didn't have his share of sexual thoughts. He was red-blooded, after all, but there was a time and place for that. Neither of which was now with this woman.

"Look, I have to insist that you don't carry on with the talking-to-animals thing around my daughter."

She stopped, her mouth open as if more words were dying to pour forth. "You don't want me to talk to Fluffy?"

"Fluffy is off-limits."

"But he's traumatized."

Unfortunately, it couldn't be helped. "No talking."

"You don't understand." Her eyes widened. "His fear will fester in his internal organs. Thoughts can do horrible things."

"Fluffy's a cat."

"Mr. Rutland. Cats are delicate creatures. We're talking about Fluffy's quality of life here. Don't you care?"

She stared at him as if he'd grown horns out of his head and started breathing fire from his nose. Any minute now, she'd be demanding to see his pitchfork. It was a terrible thing to have Lili look at him that way. As if he'd run over a cat and left it thrashing on the road while he went his merry way.

She flapped her hand at him and huffed out a weary breath. "Okay, here's the thing. I've been trying to figure out *how* to tell you, but I realize now that I'm never going to lead myself neatly into it. It has to be said."

She pursed her lips, which he was sure was a very un-Lili-like expression, and a knot tangled in his stomach. *Had* she bilked Wanetta out of the house? No. Even without Roscoe's explanation, Lili didn't fit the type. "Am I going to have to call the police?"

He was trying to make light, but she heaved a great sigh, and all the giddiness seemed to slide right off her face. As if for the last fifteen minutes, she'd been giving him a grand performance. Or maybe *this* was the performance.

"Not yet," she said without a hint of her previous vivacity. "You should sit down." She pulled a chair out and sat herself.

Not yet. That had an ominous sound. But really, how bad could it be? They were talking about a cat, for God's sake. He didn't think Lili was going to confess to murder.

Grand larceny? Maybe. But not murder.

"*I'm* the one who needs to sit down," she told him. "And I feel very nervous with you towering over me. The Bigfoot comparison, you know. Please sit?" Then she beamed.

He wasn't sure how a woman could flip from pursed lips to beaming so seamlessly, but he figured Lili Goodweather couldn't be kept down for long. Or maybe she had multiple personalities.

Her smile knocked him sideways. Her fresh scent, like spring rain and new flowers, made him dizzy. Her voice and her nonstop dialogue had thrown him off balance from the moment he'd stepped into her house. Or rather, since he'd stepped into her world, because Lili seemed to live in a completely different dimension from him.

He wasn't sure how he'd keep her smile from overriding his common sense no matter what she was about to confess.

CHAPTER THREE

"PLEASE SIT." Lili gave Tanner her most winning smile, which was difficult to do under the circumstances.

Gosh, he was tall. She was on the tall side herself at five foot eight and not used to looking so far up at a man. Tanner had to be over six feet. He looked scrumptious in jeans and a dark blue, button-down shirt. In addition, like icing on a cake, he had broad shoulders, divine true-blue eyes and hanks of gorgeous, short blond hair. Erika's was lighter, like golden threads, but her father's was a deep tan color. And thick. Yummy enough to touch. Not to mention his low, sexy voice, which had an effect like caramel sauce drizzled all over your body. Then licked off. In a past life, he was probably a Viking warrior. Not a raider, but a protector. That was how he'd talked about Erika. He adored that girl. What a big sweetie he was.

Only she didn't think he was going to be so sweet when she told him what Fluffy had witnessed.

Tanner sat. Einstein was still on the table. Glowering. Lili didn't reproach the cat aloud. She'd already let her mouth run away with her and put Tanner on the defensive. At the very least, he thought she was an airhead even if she wasn't blond.

"So, as I was saying, when I—" She cut herself off. She couldn't say *talked* with Fluffy, because talking about *talking* with animals had already gotten them off to a bad start.

Bite the bullet, babe. Her own face with a bullet between her teeth. Lili could see Einstein was going to be a problem.

Vamoose. The cat was born to be queen of the manor, and the minute she jumped down, her tail high, the flock on the kitchen floor dispersed right along with her.

Lili clasped her hands in her lap. And bit the bullet. "I discovered that Fluffy witnessed a murder sometime last night."

She expected anger. Maybe even fury. Instead, Tanner Rutland leaned an elbow on the table, covered his mouth with a big hand and looked at her with those sky-blue eyes. One one-thousand, two one-thousand. She counted up to five waiting for the inevitable explosion.

Instead, he laughed.

Tanner had issues. The poor man had a muddy-blue aura like Fluffy, but he also had a lot of gray. Gray was bad. It meant his fears, and perhaps some sort of resentment, festered inside him. The man would give himself a heart attack at an early age. Lili had a feeling he was pining for his wife. He probably had scads of messy emotions about her death, and Lili would be willing to bet he'd never talked about them. *Never.*

Right now all his muddy blue-gray had morphed into a playful bright yellow. What he needed was more laughter in his life.

Only this wasn't the time for him to be laughing.

He controlled himself, swiping a hand down his face. "Sorry, but that's the last thing I expected you to say."

"What did you expect?"

"Maybe that Bigfoot chased Fluffy."

He *was* laughing at her, and he did think she was a ditzy airhead. It didn't matter. "I wouldn't joke about it."

"I don't mean to sound doubtful. I know you believe everything you're saying."

Translation: "You may believe it but no one else in his right mind will."

She hadn't a clue how to convince him. Except to appeal to his good sense. "Haven't you seen Fluffy? He's really shaken up."

"I've seen Fluffy." And that was all he said.

"If I tell you how I talk to animals, that might explain—"

He held up a hand. "It's not necessary." Then he gave her a quizzical look, as if he were debating how to phrase his next words. "I assume you'd like to do a second reading on Fluffy."

She couldn't help smiling, glowing actually. He got it! "I can clear up everything if I spend a little more time with him. Maybe what I saw—" she spread her hands in apology "—isn't what I thought I saw." It was a possibility. Even a hope.

Tanner leaned back in his chair, crossed one running shoe–clad foot over the opposite knee and held his ankle with both hands. Then he switched, the other foot to the other knee, and took a long, *long* time to ask his next question. "How much do you charge for something like that?"

This time she gasped. "I don't charge. I *help* animals. I would never ask for anything in return."

His gaze flitted around the kitchen, then returned to hers, almost reluctantly. And she knew what he was thinking.

"I didn't *ask* Wanetta to leave me the house."

She was used to being judged crazy or silly or stupid. But no one had ever accused her of using her skills for profit. Or worse, to swindle an elderly lady out of her house.

He cleared his throat. "I'm not trying to be insulting—" *trying* being the operative word, because she was insulted. "Wanetta was sharp. She'd never let you get away with it."

"Is that the *only* reason you don't think I'm guilty?"

His gaze traveled her face, then settled on her lips, and she heated from the inside out, then the outside back in.

"Not the only reason." He raised his eyes to hers, and she was caught by the blueness. "I don't think you know how to lie."

It was a backhanded sort of compliment, but she took it anyway. "Thank you."

He dropped his voice to a husky whisper that shivered along her arms. "And Wanetta knew a good heart when she met one."

Now *that* compliment made her cheeks flush hotter than his lingering gaze on her lips.

As he sat back, the intimate moment dissolved. "How you got Wanetta's house isn't my main concern right now."

"What is?"

"I don't want my daughter involved in anything."

Her hand to her chest, she whispered, "But this is *murder.*"

He leaned forward once more, until they were so close she could see her reflection in his pupils. He smelled good, like sun-dried laundry and mellow after-shave. "Why don't you tell me exactly what—" he made a visible effort not to gulp "—you saw."

She told him everything, minus the gory descriptions, but in her mind, she could hear the awful sound of each blow.

Tanner drummed his fingers on the table for a long moment. "What is it you want me to do?"

There. That was it. What did she expect him to do? Make the problem go away? Take it off her shoulders? Yes, as feeble as it sounded, she wouldn't mind the big, strong man making everything better. She'd never realized she could be so weak. "I'd like to talk to Fluffy. If I can get him to show me where he was, then I can direct the police myself."

At least he didn't laugh. "You might have this thing wrong. The cat was purring when I left."

"He felt better after he told me." Just as she would have felt better if Tanner Rutland had said he'd take care of everything. As pitiful as that sounded.

His gaze on her, his eyes inscrutable, he said, "I'm willing to go to the police with you to tell them what you saw."

She noticed he didn't say she could tell them Fluffy saw it. "Will you back me up?"

"I don't see how I can do that."

"Because you don't believe me?"

"I can't attest to something only you saw."

Which was a diplomatic way of saying he didn't believe her. "If you don't believe me, how do you expect the police to believe me? They'll think I'm nutzoid and write the whole thing off as nonsense. I have to have some evidence to take to them first." She clasped her hands, hunched her shoulders and whispered, "Like where the body is."

Lili figured she'd rendered Tanner speechless for good this time. He opened his mouth, closed it, then closed his eyes, and finally, *finally* looked at her again. "Which means you want to talk to Fluffy again. Then you'll look for the body."

"Yes."

His fingers drummed in staccato beats. "I made a reasonable offer. We go to the police together. That's my *only* offer."

Lili digested that without a word.

"Try to see it from my point of view. If there *is* a body out there," he continued, "the last thing I'll do is allow Fluffy, and hence my daughter, to be brought into this."

"But I wouldn't—"

He held up a hand. "We'll let the police find the body. It can't take that long. That's the sensible thing to do."

She looked at him in horror. There was a dead man out there. There was a *murderer.* How could they play wait and see? She shouldn't have told him how Einstein got her name or the carnivore/Bigfoot thing. Both were a strike against her. She'd known "being herself" wasn't a good idea.

"So I can't talk to Fluffy?"

This time he gave no hesitation at all. "No, you can't talk to Fluffy. Or Erika." He shot her a stern look. "Or Roscoe."

He'd covered all the bases. She didn't blame him. He didn't want Erika involved. Either with Lili or her animal talk, or, God forbid, with murder. She could appreciate that, really she could. Yet it meant only one thing.

She'd have to find the body on her own.

THE EVENING WINDS HAD PICKED up, as they usually did around sunset. Tanner pushed his way through the opening in the driveway hedge that Erika and Roscoe had used to get over to Wanetta's house. He wondered at what point they'd all stop thinking of it as Wanetta's place instead of Lili's house. Maybe never, since Wanetta had lived there long before Erika was born.

Dealing with Lili was like starting up a subsidiary in a foreign country. The laws were completely different and required months of research.

Tanner couldn't say he one hundred percent *didn't* believe Fluffy told Lili about a murder. A person could never be one hundred percent sure of anything. A little doubt was healthy. But the odds were ninety-nine percent against her. Not that he thought Lili was a total mental case, either. She was a dreamer. In many ways, she was like his wife, like Karen. Effervescent, sweet, happy, but she didn't have both feet planted on the ground. People deluded themselves for a variety of reasons. He didn't think Lili was outright lying. She simply saw what she wanted to see and for some reason, she'd gotten it into her head that Fluffy had witnessed a murder, capitalized, underlined and bolded. Maybe it made her feel useful or worthwhile or important. He couldn't begin to guess what Lili got out of it. That would take those months of research to figure out.

Whatever emotional need Lili was filling for herself was academic at this point. While halfway through the conversation he'd been willing to allow Lili to play animal behaviorist, he drew the line at letting Erika contemplate whether her cat had actually seen a man bludgeoned to death.

When he'd set out for Lili's house, it had been to protect Erika from a silly woman's nonsense. Not quite an hour later, and with a head full of Lili's charm and sweetness, everything had become about protecting Lili...from herself.

The only way to do that was to deny her access to Fluffy.

Even if he was ninety-nine percent sure there was no body to find. Maybe *because* he was ninety-nine percent sure.

"HERE YOU GO, HONEY BUNCH." Manny pushed Lili's mocha across the countertop and took the fiver she'd laid down.

Lili snapped on a lid, squirting a dollop of whipped cream through the top hole. Not wanting to waste a smidgen, she scooped it up and licked her finger. She couldn't start a Friday—or any day—without a white mocha. Benton had only one coffeehouse, but the girls behind the counter at the Coffee Stain made the best mochas ever. Better than Manny, though with him being the Stain's owner, she'd never say that.

Manny counted out her change, then leaned forward. "Got any gossip from the animal kingdom?" It was supposed to be a whisper, but Manny was a large man and his whisper was a boom. It was rumored that he'd once been a big-time wrestler before he opened the Stain a couple of years ago. He certainly had the flattened nose as evidence. She'd offered him Pug, Wanetta's black on white with the squashed nose. Lili thought they'd be a perfect match, but Manny claimed he wasn't home enough for a cat. She wasn't giving up yet, though. After all, Pug didn't refer only to his nose; it could be short for Pugilist.

Manny always kidded her about talking to animals. It didn't bother her, honestly, but she couldn't resist giving him back his own medicine. Tit for tat, so to speak. "The only animal I've talked to today is that cockroach by the front door. He's got an army of friends on the way to meet him."

Manny frowned, then looked at the line of customers streaming to the door and the full tables behind her. "That's not funny, Lili. Besides, cockroaches aren't animals."

She patted his hand. "I was kidding. A cockroach army wouldn't take *you* on."

He wiped a drop of sweat from his brow. "Whew," he said, then boomed out, "Next!"

The Stain was packed as usual: morning commuters, moms with children getting together for a morning gab, a couple of oldsters gossiping between sips from huge cups of milky coffee. Time moved slower in Benton, and Manny usually stopped to say a few words with every customer. Lili recognized a lot of faces, but she couldn't say she knew any of them except to smile at. She shoved a couple of napkins in her Danish bag and slid her mocha into a java jacket to protect her fingers from the heat.

And started thinking about Tanner all over again as she headed to the door. Last night, it had been clear he wouldn't help her. Lili should have left that question unasked. *I can't talk to Fluffy?* If she hadn't asked, she could rationalize that he hadn't said no. As it was now, she couldn't go behind his back and ask Roscoe or Erika to help her.

It was too bad she liked Tanner. Even worse, he was hot enough to make her feel like Einstein in heat. Except that Einstein didn't have the female-heat mechanism anymore. Lili didn't do a lot of dating because, well, people could be judgmental. Somehow, her relationships—and that went for the majority of her people interactions, not just dating—were usually about what she claimed she did with animals, not about who she was as a human being. Most men she'd been out with never got past the fact that she *thought* she could talk to animals. Either they ran for the hills, or they wanted her to teach them how to talk to their pit bull. There was no happy medium. But while Tanner had semi-insulted her, he'd taken it all back with that one-liner. *Wanetta knew a good heart when she met one.*

He thought she had a good heart. Wow. But he wouldn't let her talk to Fluffy.

So, after work, she'd have to go into the woods alone, though she did feel like Little Red Riding Hood. Hopefully the Big Bad Wolf wasn't out this evening. If she thought too seriously about what could really be out there, she got…freaky. Sick and scared. It was so much better to treat what Fluffy had seen as if it were something on one of those TV forensics shows.

Maybe it *was* all a mistake. She'd made mistakes before. Still, she had an obligation to check it out. Bumping the Coffee Stain's door open with her hip, she bounded through. If she didn't hurry, she'd be late to work.

"I know what you are."

Lady Dreadlock—Lili had no clue what her real name was so she'd made one up—stood immobile on the sidewalk, right between Lili and the haven of the flower shop two doors down. A steady stream of cars passed on the road as commuters headed out to the highway; the coffeehouse doors whooshed open and closed behind her and the bank's ATM was doing a brisk business, but Lili felt isolated by the woman's dark, beady stare. Her eyes reached soul deep, and Lili suspected the woman didn't like what she saw.

The lady's once-white skin was tanned to the color of worn leather, and the sun had etched deep crags into her face that made her look twenty years older than she probably was, which, Lili guessed, was somewhere around her own age of thirty-one. Shoulder-length dreadlocks sprouted from her head like Medusa snakes. Lili couldn't tell if she was blond or the sun had simply bleached the color from her hair and eyebrows. The toes of her tennis shoes were missing, and her white socks were dingy. Despite it being a somewhat warm April day, the woman wore a vest, over a sweater, over a shirt, all covered by a raggedy coat.

"God is watching you," Lady Dreadlock intoned.

After three months of this, Lili hadn't figured out why God was watching her. She'd tried to feel empathy for the woman, who wasn't right in the head. She lived in the halfway house on the other side of town, and it was obvious that at some point she'd been homeless. She deserved Lili's sympathy. But why pick on *Lili?* The woman never asked for money, never got closer than four feet, never touched Lili. But her voice was so…there.

"Good morning. Nice seeing you. I'm going to be late for work." Lili always tried to be polite. She figured if she said *beat it,* the situation would only deteriorate.

Lady Dreadlock pointed at the sky. "God thinks we're bad."

Was that the collective "we," or Lili and the dreadlock lady?

Lady Dreadlock bent at the waist, bringing her face closer to Lili's, though without invading her personal space. "Be careful," she snapped, "or God will punish *you.*"

Then, after uttering her last enigmatic proclamation, the woman shuffled off in the opposite direction, muttering to herself, and, if she was true to form, Lili wouldn't see her for another couple of weeks. The woman never hurt her, never physically threatened her, she merely *said* things, always the same things. God was watching. God would punish. And that was about it. In three months, the refrain had not changed one iota.

Lili couldn't figure out how to help the lady. She could help cats, dogs, hamsters, rabbits, the occasional horse—though she'd never tried goldfish or snakes, and what about that infestation of carpenter ants from the oak trees around the house?—but she couldn't help Lady Dreadlock. It left Lili feeling helpless and inadequate, because she *wanted* to help.

She juggled her mocha and Danish, unlocked the front door of Flowers By Nature, scrambled inside, then locked it again until opening time. The perfume of tens of different kinds of flowers soothed her, along with the aroma of damp soil in the potted plants. She loved the scents after the store had been shut up for a night, like a jungle after

a hard rain, semidark and earthy. Plants and flowers ringed
the small shop, with a center aisle of arrangements and
two stone pathways on either side leading to the back.
With the light hum of the refrigerator units along the end
wall, it was never quiet, but Lili sometimes thought she
could almost hear the flowers talk.

"You should call the cops on that woman."

Lili shrieked and almost dropped her coffee. *That*
certainly wasn't a flower talking. "Don't scare me like
that, Kate."

Kate Carson, her boss, counted cash at the back by
the register, several blond curls escaping the stylish knot
on her head. Kate wore her hair up—it gave her three
extra inches of height above her own five foot three—
but by noon, the mass of curls would have fallen past
her shoulders.

"How can you keep track of the cash and scare me
at the same time?" Lili lost count if someone talked to
her, which was why she liked to get in early and have
everything set up before anyone else arrived for work.

"I'm an excellent multitasker." Kate also had eyes out
the back of her head. That was the only explanation for
how she'd even seen Lili with Lady Dreadlock outside
the Stain. Kate licked her index finger and started on
another stack of green bills. Her red lipstick matched her
nail polish.

Kate could rub her tummy and pat her head at the
same time. Lili couldn't. A couple of years older than
Lili, her boss was expert at a lot of things. The name
of the shop, Flowers By Nature, was Kate's brainchild,
and it was perfect. In the five years Lili had worked
for her, Kate had gone from one employee to three de-

signers, a clerk to process the phone and Internet orders, a teenager to clean and prep flowers for the cooler, two delivery guys, and besides Lili, a part-time salesgirl.

"I thought I was opening for you today." They were closed on Sundays, but Lili worked the other six days a week, though only half days on Tuesday and Saturday. She always opened the shop. Opening was her favorite time of day. "I would have brought you coffee if I'd known you'd be here."

"I felt lazy sleeping in." Kate flipped her wrist and glanced at her watch. "Had to be up early anyway. A couple of meetings, one at Swann's and another wedding. 'Tis the season."

"Ooh, you're going to Swann's." Lili waggled her eyebrows.

"Do *not* give me a look. I'm not interested in Mr. Swann."

Kate had a goal—growing her flower business—and she didn't let growing a relationship get in her way. Lili had thought about giving her one of the cats for company, but the only living things Kate wanted in her condo were of the variety that had their roots in soil. Kate dated, she liked men, but she always had her eye on the objective.

Lili thought she was missing out on a great opportunity. "He's such a hottie."

Joseph Swann had dark mahogany hair and lapis-blue eyes. Lili'd tried to see if he wore colored contact lenses or if the color was natural—because it was almost…unnatural—but she never had figured it out.

Kate straightened the stack of cash, pushed the bills into the register drawer, then stared down her nose at

Lili. Despite being shorter, it worked. "I am not, repeat *not* dating a man who touches dead people."

"Just because he runs a funeral home doesn't mean he actually touches them." Lili liked to think the crinkles at his eyes were laugh lines, but she hadn't seen him laugh much, which was expected since he dealt with grieving families all the time. That must be the worst, your whole job spent working with people who were crying, shell-shocked or inappropriately happy because Grandpa had left them a chunk of money in his will. Or mad as a rattler because he hadn't.

That didn't make Joseph Swann a bad guy. "Give him a shot."

Kate bared her teeth. "No!" Then she started on the coin count. "Now, about calling the cops."

That was the thing about Kate. You couldn't sidetrack her. She always came back to her original point if you didn't let her make it the first time.

"You know I can't call the police. If there's a whiff of trouble again at the halfway house, they'll shut the place down like they did when Elvira Gulch complained about that man peeing on her roses." It had taken six months to reopen the home after all the red tape. "Those people need a place to live." Although Lili agreed it wasn't right for him to pee on the roses.

"Her name isn't Elvira Gulch."

"But she reminds me of the wicked witch on her bicycle when she tries to take Toto to the pound. I hear that music playing every time I see her. Doo-dee-doo-dee-doo-doo."

Kate laughed. "You are so funny. But you need to do something about that woman hassling you every day."

"It's not every day. Only every couple of weeks."

Whenever the woman happened to catch her alone on the sidewalk. Lili had first encountered her while she'd been soothing a puppy's nerves when his owner had tied him to a lamppost outside the Coffee Stain. The poor little thing had been experiencing separation anxiety.

And Lady D. had started experiencing *something* toward Lili.

"It's scary," Kate said.

It wasn't so much scary as unsettling. Lili wasn't afraid. Not in an oh-my-God-she-might-have-a-meat-cleaver-in-her-purse kind of way. Lady Dreadlock didn't have a purse.

The woman didn't terrify her as much as Fluffy's images slamming into her mind had done. That was something she had to take care of ASAP. Or at least before the sun went down. "Can I leave a little early today, Kate? I've got some errands I want to run, and I don't like riding my bike home after dark."

"At least you're sensible about *something,* and yes, I can lock up tonight." Kate was the *best* boss.

"Thanks." Lili scuttled past into the back room before Kate could return to talk of the dreadlock lady. The back area was much bigger than the front of the shop since that's where the majority of the work was done and the flowers were stored.

"You're avoiding the issue," Kate's voice followed.

Lili set down her coffee and Danish. The issue. What was the issue? Lady D.? Or Fluffy and what he'd seen? Or Tanner Rutland and what he wasn't willing to do about it?

She poked her head out the door. "Can I ask a question?"

Kate glanced over her shoulder. "You can ask

whatever you want. After I hear it, I'll decide whether I want to answer."

"Deal." She took a deep breath and spilled the whole story. "Erika Rutland is the girl who lives next door to me, and her cat saw a murder in the woods, and the body hasn't been discovered yet, so I can't go to the police because they won't believe me unless I find the body, but Tanner—that's Erika's father—won't let me talk to the cat or Erika about it, so I have no idea where the body is, and what would you do in my place?"

Kate smacked a roll of quarters on the counter and poured them into the cash drawer. "How old is this Tanner guy?"

"Thirty-five, thirty-seven, something like that."

"Is he a hottie?"

He was definitely a hottie—better than funeral director Joseph Swann—but Lili didn't see what that had to do with Fluffy and the murder. "*Hottie* would be a good word to describe him."

"Then it's easy." Kate lifted a shoulder. "Seduce him."

"Seduce him?"

"He'll be putty in your hands."

"Hmm. I never would have thought of that." That was what Lili admired about Kate. She thought outside the box. And she didn't even ask for further details on a pretty darn convoluted story. Lili wasn't sure if Kate actually believed she could talk to animals, but that was the other great thing about her boss. Kate never judged. She was a go-with-the-flow kind of person. Except about Joseph Swann's career choice.

"I'm full of amazing ideas." Kate raised one perfectly penciled eyebrow. "And modest, too."

"I bow to your genius. Guess that's why you're the boss."

It might work. If she didn't find anything out in the woods when she went for her hike after work, she'd seduce Tanner Rutland into giving her access to Fluffy.

With Tanner, the idea had certain exciting side benefits.

Lili ducked through the door in search of her Danish and coffee.

Kate's voice pursued her. "And don't do anything silly like traipsing out into the woods to search for a body on your own."

Darn. Why did Kate have to bring up common sense?

CHAPTER FOUR

"THAT CONCLUDES OUR BUSINESS. How about lunch?"

Joseph Swann was tricky. He never asked her on a date, but over the last couple of months, he'd slipped invitations in as part of their business arrangements. Kate Carson wasn't fooled. He was after her for more than a spinach salad. She was flattered, but the man was a no-go.

"Thanks, but I've got another meeting right after this." Besides, she had to get back to Flowers By Nature. Lili had her a trifle worried over this latest animal communiqué. While not a careless person in the main, Lili had an obsession with helping animals, which sometimes blinded her to everything else.

Kate busied herself putting her files back in her briefcase. Joseph Swann didn't make her nervous, nor did his office. There was nothing particularly funereal in it. He sat behind a standard dark wood desk, something rich-looking but not too rich. His chair was leather, but well used. There were filing cabinets along the wall and bookcases filled with compendiums whose titles she'd never bothered to look at. Instead of a conference-style table, he had a black leather sofa, two matching chairs and a coffee table. The corner of the room housed a small coffee stand with ceramic mugs rather than foam cups.

And though pastel watercolors on the walls soothed, as did the blue-gray carpet, it wasn't as if he had piped-in organ music or brochures of caskets on the table.

He steepled his fingers, rested them against his lips and eyed her over the tops. "You're lying." His voice had a soft, almost singsong quality to it, as if he were amused by her continued efforts to resist his invitations.

She didn't expect him to be so open about it, but it was exactly what she *should* have expected from him. Joseph Swann was actually witty and charming, soft-spoken as befitted his profession, and devilishly handsome. His most stunning feature was his square jawline. Kate couldn't say why it fascinated her more than his mahogany hair or his lapis-blue eyes, to use Lili's description. Kate had to admit the man was sexy with a six-foot, well-maintained body, as far as one could tell on someone who primarily wore dark suits with the jacket buttoned, a white dress shirt and a charcoal-striped tie. It was that jawline that did it for her. Strength, maybe that was it. Whatever. The problem between them was not his jaw; it was the whole dead-people issue. Though he often made her laugh, a man who spent the majority of his time around dead bodies couldn't be normal.

She gave him a prissy, prim stare to mask the smile that threatened. "I am not lying, and I resent your saying that."

He smiled. "No, you don't. You think it's entertaining that I keep asking even after you've turned me down…what?" He spread his hands. "Five times?"

"Six, counting this one." She couldn't help the answering smile. If only he didn't do what he did. He also struck her as a relationship kind of man, which didn't fit her life plan.

"Maybe I should have told you right up front that I'm not into necrophilia."

She snorted. He really was amusing. At first, she hadn't thought he'd had a sense of humor at all, especially considering his career selection, but little by little, she'd realized he had a droll wit that caught up with you a few lines later.

"I don't have sex with dead people. I prefer live women."

Kate outright laughed. "Prefer?"

"Maybe I should have used another word. I like women who are of the living, breathing variety."

She'd worked with him two years; he was one of her best customers. While many of the bereaved wanted to handle the flower arrangements themselves, some wanted everything done by the funeral home, an "I can't bear to think about that now" mentality that Kate understood completely. She knew he wasn't hers exclusively; he used plenty of other florists, but she did feel she got special hands-on attention, especially over the last couple of months. And he always threw in a few zingers during their dealings. Probably to let her know *he* was a live one. Versus a dead one. This conversation, however, took the cake. "Is this like cop humor, making a joke out of a morbid thing?"

"I don't think what I do is morbid."

"You work with dead people." Her voice rose a tad with incredulity. "That's morbid."

"I primarily work with their loved ones. It's a very different thing."

"Yes, but—"

He held up his hand. "Why don't we talk over lunch, get it all out in the open and ease your fears about it?"

"I don't have fears about it."

"Yes, you do."

"Now you sound more like a psychiatrist than a mortician."

"I'm not a mortician. I'm a funeral director. See, there's your first misconception. And funeral directors do need to have a handle on the psychology of the situation. I've been to a few seminars on dealing with the emotional end of the business."

"Mr. Swann—"

"You always call me *mister* when I'm trying to ask you out."

"I'm not dating you." Then she realized that was a bit too strong. "I'm concentrating on the flower business right now. Dating is low on my list of priorities."

He went on as if she hadn't even spoken. "Most women fall into two categories. Either they're utterly fascinated with what I do, want to hear every dirty detail, and sometimes I think *they're* into necrophilia, especially when they ask me not to move during…uh…certain activities."

She covered her eyes, inhaled a deep breath and laughed again. He was irresistible in a rubber-necker kind of way. "I'm not one of those women."

"Then there's the other kind. They're terrified something might rub off on them. Fear of dying and all that."

"I'm not that kind, either."

"Then go out with me."

"I don't have time for dating. I've got a business."

He shrugged. "All right, I'll settle for sex. I promise not to ask you to do it in the embalming room or in a coffin."

She wanted to roll on the floor laughing. It was the most surreal conversation she'd had in her life. Except when her mother had made Kate accompany her to the funeral home to make arrangements for her inevitable passing. "Mr. Swann—"

"At least call me Joe."

"All right, Joe. We've worked together for two years. Why are you pushing this *now?*"

"The nesting instinct. It'll sneak up on you. You'll see some stranger walking down the street and bam, it'll hit you. Before you know it, you'll be dating him, then marriage, then children. I see you with—" he shrugged, eyeing her "—two. I want to make sure you give me a chance before you meet him."

Where did the man come up with the idea? About *her,* of all people? "That is the most ridiculous thing I've ever heard."

He spread his hands. "Is it?"

"I don't have a mothering bone in my body." She was a driven businesswoman like her mother. But her mother had succumbed to the biological-clock tick when she was thirty-eight. She hadn't needed a husband, though she had wanted a child. That wasn't going to happen to Kate, but she steered clear of the future family-man type to be sure.

He smiled. "Then just having sex is fine by me."

She found him attractive and funny, but his profession—yuck. "It's not a good idea to have sex with my biggest customer."

"You have an answer for everything."

"You're right. I do. I'm exceptionally flattered, though."

"I haven't given up. I will keep asking."

"No means no, Joe."

"If you'd said I made your skin crawl, I'd be willing to accept that no means no. But you didn't."

"Is that all I have to do?"

"Yes."

She thought about it. She really, really did. But he didn't make her skin crawl, far from it. She wasn't that mean or unfeeling to actually say that out loud, anyway. Maybe she enjoyed the chase, too. Not that she'd give in, but as long as he knew the score up front, what was the harm? "No—" she put a finger over her lips "—means no."

"It's only a matter of time before you succumb."

Cocky bastard. Still, she liked him. She wouldn't date him or have sex with him, but she liked him nonetheless.

APRIL WAS USUALLY A RAINY month, but this year hadn't brought the typical deluge, so the meadow was dry, the late evening sun was warm and the breeze whispered through the long grasses. For the first time ever, the soft shush raised goose bumps along Lili's arms, and she kept looking behind her as if Fluffy's murderer would jump out of a gopher hole. Though she hadn't bothered to change her skirt, she'd worn her hiking boots in case she stepped into one of those cavities. Boots helped avoid a sprained ankle.

She realized now, she wanted to avoid a lot more than that. Meadow, forest, oak tree. That was what Fluffy had shown her. She'd made it to the middle of the meadow, then gotten scared. Actually, she'd been scared when she'd left her house, tramped through her backyard and hit one of the narrow trails that wound through the trees. To the south, east and west, the semicircle of surrounding houses was separated from the meadow by a ring of forest that took a few minutes to traverse. To the north, it was woods all the way to the summit. As the crow flies, most of the houses were well within walking distance, even Buddy Welch's. Luckily, she'd never seen him out here. Sometimes she wondered if he was nothing more than an urban legend. Then again, encountering Buddy Welch was better than scanning for—gulp—vultures flying overhead. She didn't want to find a body, not now, not ever, at least not while she was alone.

"This is really stupid," she whispered to herself. Seducing Tanner Rutland into letting her communicate with Fluffy was a darn sight better than trying it on her own.

Several yards away, Einstein's tail cleared the waving stalks as she jumped at something, probably a gopher poking its head up. It was said that you couldn't walk a cat the way you could walk a dog, but Einstein often accompanied her on hikes. She also quickly disappeared when something caught her fancy. Even as Lili tried to keep her eye on it while she walked, the cat's tail was swallowed up by the long grass.

Her boot caught on something. Then she tripped. Over a body. And screamed.

And kept on screaming when it sat up.

"I know what you are," it droned as it rose to its feet.

Lili started to breathe again. It wasn't a dead body, it wasn't a ghost. Not even Bigfoot.

It was Lady D. Normally Lili would have been nervous, but when she'd been terrified she'd tripped over a real body, tripping over Lady Dreadlock was the lesser of two evils.

"It's a gorgeous day, isn't it?" Lili rolled to her hands and knees, then got to her feet and backed up several steps. She didn't feel comfortable with the woman standing over her. Her relief at not having tripped over a real body quickly receded. It was bad enough seeing the woman in town, but out here…alone? It was creepy. Where was Einstein? And what was the woman doing out in the wide open spaces when her usual haunts were in town?

"God is watching you," Lady D. said, her usual refrain.

Lili almost mouthed the woman's next words aloud, but the empty meadow was way too empty to start antagonizing her. "It's a lovely day for a hike."

"God thinks we're bad." She pointed at the darkening sky.

Standing alone in the middle of the field with nothing around but big trees and long grass and the sky overhead, Lili wished she'd reported the woman the way Kate had told her to.

Could dreadlocks look like a helmet from a cat's-eye view? Actually, no. Not in any way, shape or form could the woman's hair be covered by a bowl-shaped helmet the size Fluffy had seen.

"Be careful or God will punish *you*." This time, Lady D. pointed her finger at Lili, her fingernail short and ragged.

Maybe it was the quiet, the lack of traffic and passersby, or the fact that her last mocha had been about nine hours ago, but Lili couldn't take it anymore. She didn't care about being polite or nonconfrontational. She cared about the empty meadow, but if the woman was going to threaten her, she had to at least know why. "What do you know? You always say that, and you never tell me *why*. What have I done that God's so mad at?"

The woman smiled, the leathery texture of her skin creasing her mouth and deepening the grooves meandering down her face, then she stared at something over Lili's shoulder. "Ask the cat."

The cat? In three months, it was the first thing the woman had ever said that wasn't part of her script. Lili wanted to hear more, but Lady Dreadlock turned and glided away.

"Wait. What's that supposed to mean?"

Lady D. ignored Lili, trailing her fingers along the tops of the grass, until she reached the edge of the forest and it sucked her into its depths.

Einstein appeared, sitting down in the trampled grass.

"Where have you been?" Lili almost shrieked.

Important things to do. An image of a field mouse popped into Lili's mind.

Lili simply plopped down in the middle of the grass and closed her eyes. "This was a stupid idea." She cracked one eye open. "And don't you dare give me the dunce cap."

Einstein yawned. Which *was* better than the dunce cap.

"If there is something out here, I shouldn't be looking for it by myself."

Einstein lifted a paw and licked the pad.

"What do you think she was doing out here?" Then she flashed an image of the dreadlocked woman.

I'm a cat. How would I know? For once, Einstein gave herself the dunce cap.

"Well, *she* told me to ask you." What did that mean, anyway?

Einstein merely blinked. She couldn't figure out Lady Dreadlock, either.

Lili sighed and wrapped her arms around her knees. "Do you think we could be wrong about what Fluffy saw?" *We?*

Then Lili rolled to her feet. "There's only one thing to do." Whatever was necessary to get Tanner Rutland on her side. "I'll have to seduce him."

Einstein started a hacking cough.

"I was kidding."

Liar, liar, pants on fire. She saw an image of a woman cupping the rear of her burning jeans. "Let's go home. I'll think about it all later." After a salad and a cherry cordial chocolate kiss.

Einstein hunkered in the trampled grass. *She spammed me.*

Einstein was like a shadow, following Lili everywhere, often sitting at Lili's computer while she downloaded her e-mail. In between her weekly calls to her parents, that's how Lili kept in touch. For every one real e-mail, she got twenty spam, which she vociferously complained about. Einstein knew what spam was.

Lili put her hands on her hips. "*Who* did *what?*"

Flashing SPAM can images this time, and a likeness of Lady Dreadlock.

"She talked to you while you were hiding in the grass?" *Didn't I say that?* Einstein flumped onto her side.

"Don't do that. I'm going to have to pick all the burrs out of your fur." She'd have to do it anyway since Einstein had been chasing field mice for half an hour. "What did she say?"

Something about the fires of hell. And you. The image

was so clear, Lili almost felt the fire up her skirt. "She imaged you like I do?"

If a cat could sigh, that was what Einstein did with a slow, weary exhalation of breath. *Humans. Yes!*

The fires of hell didn't clarify anything more than what Lady Dreadlock had already said. But that wasn't the important thing. "She talks to animals."

If Lili had figured that out on the sidewalk outside the coffeehouse with a crowd of coffee drinkers milling around her, she'd have been ecstatic. But alone in a field two days after Fluffy had seen something awful happen, Lili was sure the fires of hell weren't something she wanted to know anything about.

TANNER GOT HOME FROM WORK later than he'd intended, which happened far more often than not. A meeting ran late; a report had to go out; there was always something. Tonight, however, he had a date, and if he didn't hurry, by the time he'd changed, his car would be blocked in the driveway. Friday was pinochle night, and though Roscoe's friends all lived in the neighborhood, Chester brought them over in his ancient car for the weekly game. One of these days, the old man was going to have to give up driving, hopefully sooner rather than later.

Tanner had pulled in alongside the garage and was climbing out of his car when he saw her through the hedge. Lili pushed open the gate and tramped into her yard. From the woods. Her bright skirt was like a beacon through the hedge bushes. He'd planted the hedge a couple of years ago to separate the yards, but there were gaps that hadn't grown in completely.

Tanner found one of those gaps and pushed through

to head her off before she could get to the house. Her boots were dusty and her socks stabbed through with stickers. Her long, dark tresses had a few stickers, too, and she'd wrapped her arms around her abdomen in an almost defensive posture.

"What were you doing out there?"

She jumped. Concentrating on her feet, she hadn't seen him. But she recovered quickly. "Out where?"

All innocence. Tanner wasn't fooled. Dammit. "You were searching for the body, weren't you?"

She rolled her lips between her teeth, looked down at the cat standing beside her with its fur all ruffled up, then let her gaze pass over the kitchen door, the stoop, the ten feet between her and it. Anywhere but at him. "Not exactly."

Tanner took a deep breath to maintain control. He didn't want to flip out on her, but the woman pushed all his buttons. "What does 'not exactly' mean?"

Finally, she looked right at him. "It means that if I saw something while I was walking, I could tell the police about it."

Tanner circled, stopping with his back to her while he took deep belly breaths, then finally turned to face her. "Have you no sense, woman?" He held up his hands. "Sorry. That didn't come out right."

But it was exactly what he meant. He had doubts about whether she could talk to Fluffy. Or Einstein. Or any other nonhuman organism on the face of the planet. He required concrete proof, such as the body she said was out there. Not that he wanted Lili to find it. But *she* didn't have doubts. She believed she could talk to animals. Which meant she'd wandered in the woods knowing full well she could stumble across a dead man, or worse, the killer who had done the deed. Lili, the little idiot, had knowingly put herself in an extremely dangerous situation. Didn't she have a jot of common sense?

Jesus. She was like Karen in so many ways, with outlandish ideas that spelled trouble. If Karen hadn't been sure she had powerful psychic talents that only needed to be nurtured to come to full potency, if she hadn't been driving to Sedona to find all that nurturing, if she hadn't expressly defied his wishes, if she hadn't…

"Okay." Lili's voice pulled him back from the brink. "Here's the thing." She gulped as if she needed to find courage. "I got scared out there and decided that it was dumb to be by myself, so I came back before I started looking for a body."

Thank God Lili had *some* sense. "Don't ever do that again."

She scared him half to death even as she made him think about things he'd relegated to a place deep inside that he rarely allowed himself access to. He couldn't allow it now. What the hell concern was it of his what Lili Goodweather did?

He was, however, in touch with his inner guy enough to know that if it had been Viola the postal lady he'd seen walking out of the woods, he wouldn't have gotten angry.

"Even Einstein told me it was stupid, and she should know since she's—"

"Yeah, I know, the reincarnation of the smartest man in history." He ran a hand through his hair, and his tie felt too tight around his neck.

"I didn't go very far," she added. "Honest."

He tapped his foot, and dirt puffed up from the scrubby grass, coating his dress shoe. "How far did you go?"

"Fifteen minutes, maybe." But she looked at the sky, and he figured that fifteen minutes had stretched to half an hour.

She needed a keeper. "That's too far."

She rolled her eyes. "Believe me, I know. I'm not doing *that* again." Then she looked at him with a hint of mistiness in her eyes. "They were supposed to be *my* woods, and I've never been scared out there before. They've always been welcoming."

"Innocence lost," he murmured, then admitted the truth to himself. There was an air of innocence about her that called to him. The way she used five sentences to say something that anyone else could have said in one. The way her thoughts rolled off her tongue. The way her fluttery skirts exemplified her personality, light and whimsical. When she wasn't being idiotic.

"What did you say?"

"Nothing." He wished for a moment that she hadn't moved in next door. He had a date tonight, and his dates were with levelheaded women who weren't anything like Lili. Watching the fading sunlight play through her hair, casting it with shades of moonlit-blue and midnight-black, he found himself wanting the women he dated to be more like Lili.

"Promise you won't go on walks by yourself looking for bodies." It was his duty to give her one last reminder. "And you'll let the police handle it."

"I'll let the police handle it," she parroted.

"And you won't talk to Fluffy again."

"I won't." She put her hands behind her back.

"Let me see your fingers. I want to make sure you're not crossing them."

She held up both hands, then zipped her lip. "I won't say a word to Fluffy. Or Erika. Or Roscoe. Is there anyone else I shouldn't tell? You'd better get it all out. Maybe I should get a pad of paper and write it down." Then she covered her mouth. "Oops, I just remembered. I already told my boss."

He realized he'd been talking to her as if she were Erika's age, and condescendingly, too. Instead of getting mad, she was making fun of him. He raised one brow. "And what did he say?"

"*She* said I needed to use common sense."

"My kind of woman." Sensible.

Lili didn't say anything at all to that.

"Now that we've got that settled…" He glanced at his watch. He'd be late, yet an odd reluctance to leave her kept him rooted to the spot.

"Is there something else you wanted to tell me not to do? Speak now or forever hold your peace and all that stuff."

What he wanted to do was spend the evening with her instead of his date, Anna, an accountant. "I have a date."

She tipped her head. "That seems like a non sequitur."

It was, as far as Lili was concerned, not being privy to his inner thoughts. At least she couldn't read them as she claimed she could read animal thoughts. "I've got a date tonight, but I want to make sure you'll be okay by yourself before I leave."

"I've been living on my own for a while now. And I can scream very loudly, so if the bogeyman or Bigfoot shows up at my door, I'll be sure to wake the dead."

As long as it wasn't the body lying out there some-where in the woods. Next thing you know, she'd be saying *it* could walk. Yet he still didn't leave.

After a beat of silence, she asked, "Did you get flowers for your date? Women love flowers."

"She's not that kind of woman."

"Every woman is that kind of woman. Wait here a minute." She skipped around him in those hiking boots, puffs of dirt floating up and getting caught in little eddies by the breeze.

"I need to get out of here," he told himself as the screen door banged behind her. Yet he didn't want to. He'd known Anna for a little over a year. He'd dated her three times and slept with her once. He wasn't in love with her; she wasn't in love with him. He wasn't looking for a replacement for Karen or a mother for Erika. Not that he was afraid of emotional attachment as Roscoe often claimed, but neither was he into celibacy.

Yet being around Lili made him feel casual sex should be a little more than casual. And that was the scariest damn thought.

CHAPTER FIVE

LILI BOUNDED BACK OUT the door with a flower vase
stuck in the center circular frame of a cardboard holder.

"I made them this afternoon during a lull," she said.

"They're…" Tanner couldn't think of an appropriate
description. "Interesting?" It sounded like a question.

"I'm not a designer, but I like to tinker." She held up
the vase for his inspection. "I'm a good tinkerer, don't
you think?"

"Absolutely." He'd never seen the like. A profusion
of color, the blooms themselves were exotic and uniden-
tifiable.

"They're wildflowers. I picked them myself." She
shrugged. "My boss, Kate, says I'm going to be arrested
one day for picking contraband, but I didn't take any
California poppies. Now that would be illegal."

"What are they?"

She clucked her tongue. "Looking up the names
would take the fun out of it." Light sparkled through the
green glass and water as she held it up to the fading sun.
"Analyzing takes away from the pure enjoyment. This
way it's artistic."

"Very artistic." The arrangement, though some
people could say she'd simply plopped a bunch of

blossoms in water, was like Lili, imaginative, unusual and vibrant. He didn't think Anna would fully appreciate it. "Ah, thanks."

She placed his hand flat beneath the cardboard and tinkered with the flowers. She didn't look up, but her touch robbed him of speech and sent a flash of primal heat rushing through his body. She certainly had an effect on his base nature. He needed to get his head out of his—

"There. Perfect."

Oh yeah, she was. He had forgotten why he'd been angry when he'd seen her entering her backyard. Rather, he didn't give a damn. Two stickers were trapped in her hair. Balancing the flower vase, he plucked the first one from her silky locks. Her pupils changed, grew slightly larger. The other sticker took longer to pull free, and her breath sighed from her lips. His own was stuck in his throat.

"Thank you," she said with a hint of huskiness.

"How much do I owe you for the flowers?" It seemed the safest thing to say.

She flapped her hand. "Don't be silly. But let her think it was really expensive because it's so unique. Women like it when they think you've spent a lot of money on them."

Did *she* like expensive gifts? "You know a lot about women."

She tapped her temple. "Hello! I *am* a woman."

"I know." God, did he know.

Just then, the cat, whom Tanner had forgotten, stretched up along Lili's side, its sheathed claws reaching to the high point on her thigh. It was one damn long cat.

Lili stroked its head. "I do not have a can of SPAM."

She glanced at Tanner. "Einstein's got SPAM on the brain right now."

Tanner had things on his brain, too. Like carnivores and Bigfoot having her for dinner. Tanner wanted her for dessert.

"Thanks for the flowers," he said, backing away.

"Let me know what your date thinks."

He hadn't a single desire to go out on his date tonight. He didn't want Anna. He had condoms in the glove box, and he knew he wasn't going to even open the drugstore bag.

Yesterday, going to see Lili had been about what he thought Erika did and didn't need in her life. Twenty-four short hours later, it was about Lili and what *he* wanted from *her.*

He needed to get out of Lili's backyard.

"THAT WAS WEIRD," Lili whispered to Einstein as Tanner pushed through the hedge wall.

Actually, it was stimulating. Her heart raced in her chest and her toes tingled. Like the adrenaline rush of a bad fright. Or the moment Tanner had said he had a date.

Not that she was jealous. Tanner wasn't interested in a woman like her. She babbled too much and talked to animals. Not that she was interested in Tanner Rutland, either, no matter how deliciously tall, good-looking, loyal, commanding, blond or blue-eyed he was. He thought she was wacky. She'd had enough of that from men, enough of it from people in general. Lili patted her side as she moved up the stoop. Einstein followed.

SPAM, SPAM, SPAM.

"I told you I don't have any SPAM." Though Einstein

might be talking about Lady Dreadlock and her spam mind-mail. What did it mean? Lili didn't have an answer.

She opened the kitchen door and was almost bowled over by the cat milieu. She should have fed them before she went out, but she'd been afraid it would get dark before she completed her mission. Rita sat down in the middle of the floor and yowled.

"That is so undignified. Rita Hayworth would never make that noise." With a leopard-spotted coat, Rita was the sleek personification of the movie star she'd named herself for. Except when she yowled.

Lili started popping tops and scooping food onto plates. The cats attacked the food the minute she set it on the floor. No matter how intelligent animals were, they reverted to base instinct when they were hungry.

"You know, I've got an idea," Lili mused. "I promised Tanner *I* wouldn't talk to Roscoe or Erika or Fluffy, but I didn't promise *you* wouldn't."

Einstein flashed the universal *stop* symbol even as she happily munched away.

"I know it didn't work before. But if at first you don't succeed, try, try again." Yeah, the idea was good. "Tonight we go see Fluffy in his house." She shook her finger at Einstein. "Do not talk about emasculation or superior female intelligence."

She waited until Tanner backed his car out of the driveway next door, then a big Lincoln pulled in, the engine knocking and pinging for a few minutes after a trio of elderly men climbed from the car.

Darn. Roscoe was having guests. But a good idea was one that couldn't be ignored. Lili headed out.

Erika answered the door. "Lili, I'm so glad you're here."

Princess emblazoned her fuchsia T-shirt, and pigtails secured her long blond tresses. But those dark circles under her eyes looked almost like purple bruises.

"Is Fluffy okay?"

Erika pulled Lili inside the front hall with a strength that belied her thin arms. "He was okay until Grandpa got out the card table, but he's totally freaked now."

With *do something* written all over her, her slender body practically pulsated with anxiety. Lili's heart dropped to her toes. "Can Einstein come in, too?"

"Only if we don't tell Dad."

Lili zipped her lips. "I won't." Jeez, not even two seconds into her plan, she was already conspiring against Tanner.

A set of stairs lay straight ahead, open double doors on one side of the hardwood hall, and another set on the other side through which Lili could hear the rumble of male voices. The scent of appetizers wafted into the hall along with the voices.

"Grandpa's having his pinochle party." Erika looked at the door, then back to Lili. "There's Linwood and Chester and Hiram. Linwood's a Korean War hero, and he wears his uniform, so don't look like you think that's dumb." She waited for Lili to nod. "Chester was almost a famous movie star once, so when he says he made a movie with Deanna Durbin, pretend you know who she is."

"What if he asks me what movie she was in?"

"He won't, trust me. And Hiram wrote a very important novel, so act like you've heard of it. Dad says they're tall stories, except for Hiram. He really did write a book once. But it makes them all happy if you look excited when they tell you about it. So pretend if you have to. It's good for them."

What a sweet sentiment. Most adults wouldn't appreciate that, let alone a child of twelve. Erika was exceptional.

Lili smiled. "I won't even have to pretend."

Einstein drifted through the open door like a wisp of smoke the elderly men probably wouldn't even notice.

Erika leaned in and whispered, "Fluffy's behind the couch," then called loud enough to echo in Lili's ears, "Grandpa, Lili's here." How could children do that, generate so much volume with such a small body? Erika dragged her into the room.

"Lili, my dear." Roscoe smiled, his eyes crinkling at the corners and the grooves deepening by his mouth. "You just missed Tanner. I hope you two had a good conversation last night. I've been telling him he needed to get over there to meet you."

Ha, she'd been right. Roscoe had fibbed yesterday when he'd said Tanner couldn't *wait* to meet her. "I adored meeting him. He's the most fascinating man." She hoped that wasn't laying it on too thick, even if it was the truth.

Then she had a sudden thought. What if Erika and Roscoe told Tanner she'd come over for a visit? He'd think she talked to them about the murder against his wishes. *Hello, why didn't you think of that before?* Too late now; it would only arouse suspicion if she asked them not to tell.

"Come and meet the boys. They love pretty young women."

Elderly men did, unless they were curmudgeons. "Thank you for saying I'm pretty."

Roscoe took her arm. A large stone fireplace dominated the room, with an old-fashioned rag rug in front of the hearth and an easy chair to one side facing the TV. The heavy wood coffee table had been pushed back to make space in the center of the room for a card table, four folding chairs and another smaller table laden with plates and drinks. Erika dashed around them to fling herself on the couch beneath the window, hanging over the back to croon for Fluffy.

As if he were presenting her to the King—or kings— of England, Roscoe ushered Lili forward to the trio of elderly gentlemen grazing off plates piled high with food.

"Gentlemen, I've got a special treat for you. This is our new neighbor, Lili Goodweather."

"Linwood Daniels, at your service."

Over a pair of brown polyester slacks, Linwood wore a short brown jacket like the one she'd seen Eisenhower wear in war documentaries on the History Channel. The left front dripped with an impressive array of ribbons and medals, but the buttonholes stretched to full capacity and then some over his equally impressive belly.

He grabbed her hand and pumped it in his meaty grip. "You are a delight, a feast for the eyes." A neat band of frosty white hair circled his head from ear to ear, and a thick beard covered his chin. He looked like a Santa Claus.

His eyes were a tad hazy with cataracts, so Lili wasn't exactly sure how he could tell she was a feast for the eyes. "That's so sweet, thank you."

"Let her go, Linwood," Roscoe said, then drew her to the middle man. "Chester Pawson."

With the same white fringe of hair, he was also in his midseventies, though with fifty less pounds on him, not counting the medals, than Linwood Daniels. Chester stared at her in wide, green-eyed wonder and picked up the hand Linwood had released, giving a gentlemanly brush of a kiss on the back. "You look like Deanna Durbin. I made a movie with her back in the heyday. It was destined to be a classic. We knew it even then." He cocked his head at Roscoe. "What did you say her name is?"

"Lili Goodweather." Then Roscoe whispered in her ear, "Every woman he meets looks like Deanna Durbin."

"It's such a wonderful compliment, Mr. Pawson. Deanna Durbin was magnificent." She hadn't a clue but didn't care as Chester's eyes glowed. He squeezed her hand. "She was incomparable," Lili added.

"Oh, she was, she was. I was only seventeen at the time, but I will never forget those glorious days. If it weren't for her encouragement, my career would never have gotten off the ground."

Lili was afraid it hadn't gotten off the ground at all, so all she did was smile. Chester squeezed her hand harder. He had remarkable strength for his age. "Say, aren't you the young lady who talks to animals? We've seen you at the Coffee Stain."

It was Lili's turn to flush pink. Lord. She realized now the two oldsters she'd seen that very morning at the Stain were none other than Linwood and Chester. "Ah, yes. That's me."

"Lili's here to talk to Fluffy." Erika beamed. "He had a bad fright Wednesday night, and Lili's giving him therapy."

"That's enough about Fluffy until we've finished the introductions. Drop her hand, Chester," Roscoe ordered. "Last but not least, this is Professor Hiram Battle."

A tall beanpole of a man, he shook Lili's hand with so much vigor, her teeth almost rattled in her head. "Nice meeting," he said in abbreviated reply.

"You, too. You're a professor up at the college?"

"University." He rubbed his fingers in his steel-wool cap of hair. "College implies either a technical school or something of the junior variety."

Translation: something of inferior quality.

Lili decided not to mention that she hadn't attended either university or college. That hadn't been in her life plan. Not that she had a real life plan. "Erika tells me you've written a book. That's marvelous."

"It's a literary novel, required reading in many halls of higher education."

"That's wonderful." Then she edged around them before she made a mistake and backed toward Erika on the couch. "It's so nice meeting all of you, but don't let me disturb you. I'm going to see how Fluffy's doing. He hasn't been feeling well."

"That's because he pinched a Vienna sausage right off Roscoe's table. I saw him," Linwood said. "Then he dragged it behind the couch like a pirate with his booty."

"That's crap, Linwood. He's been behind the couch since I got out the card table, which was before I put the sausages out."

"Then it must have been a rat. A long, gray thing. You'd better tell your son to get rid of the rats. I hate rats."

Oops. It wasn't a rat. It was Einstein. That naughty cat.

Chester jumped into the fray. "Skunks are worse. You ever had one blow off outside your window? Enough to gag a maggot."

Linwood snorted. "Maggots don't gag."

"It's an expression, you old fart."

"There are no rats in this house," Roscoe declared.

"Gentlemen, are we going to play cards or are you three going to duke it out all night?" Hiram pulled out a chair and folded his beanpole frame into it, his knees almost hitting the table. Then he pinched a sausage and popped it in his mouth.

"You shuffle the pack, Hiram." Roscoe unboxed a deck and fanned them, the numbers and suits on the cards oversize, probably in deference to Linwood's cataracts. Then he straightened them again and handed the pack to Hiram. "I'll get the rest of the appetizers before they burn."

"You didn't make those taquito things again, did you? They gave me the runs last time."

Roscoe threw his hands wide. "Linwood, there are ladies present. We don't talk about the runs in front of ladies."

Lili plopped down on the couch beside Erika and whispered, "Are they always like this?"

"Pretty much. Dad always seems to have a date on the Friday nights they come over."

Lili could see why. The four old gentlemen would drive Tanner batty, but their bickering back and forth brought a smile to her lips. If they could bicker, they were alive and well.

"Now, let's see to Fluffy."

At the long, low, incessant growl, she peeked over the back of the couch. Fluffy crouched at one end, the fur along his back sticking straight up. At the other end, Einstein licked her chops, probably getting the last of the Vienna sausage off her cat mustache. Between them sat a herd of dust bunnies and a book that must have fallen off the back of the sofa.

Lili flashed a question mark. Einstein sent it back. Which meant the two cats weren't having the meaningful conversation Lili wanted. Then Einstein peeled back her lips and sneezed, stampeding the herd of dust bunnies straight at Fluffy.

Fluffy growled louder.

"What's his aura look like?" Erika asked.

"Muddy again," Lili said. "He's had a relapse. Did you keep him in last night?"

"Dad said I could. He seemed all right when I let him out this morning, and he was even okay when I got home. But Grandpa set up for the card party, and Fluffy got freaky again." Erika chewed her bottom lip and rubbed one hand up and down her thigh.

Roscoe entered with a tray of tasty-scented goodies. "Don't eat the taquitos, Linwood. Then you'll be fine."

"But they're calling to me," Linwood whined.

"Use willpower." And the card game began in earnest. Erika turned to Lili.

"Can you talk to Fluffy again?"

Lili didn't want to lie, nor did she want to break her promise to Tanner. "Let's give Einstein and Fluffy time for some feline interaction. It might garner more information." When Erika looked doubtful, Lili added, "Einstein's good at this." She puckered her brow. "We should have called her Freud."

The corner of Erika's mouth lifted, but it wasn't enough for Lili. The child needed distraction while

Einstein worked her feline magic. Leaning over the back of the couch, Lili grabbed the book that had fallen there, probably years ago. Lili had come across treasures she thought lost forever when she'd cleaned out her little apartment to move into Wanetta's house.

"Molly's New Mom," she read the title.

Erika snatched the book out of her hand and sat on it. "That's not mine. A friend of mine was over, and she must have put it on the back of the sofa, and it fell off. She'll be so glad to get it back."

Lili noted that Erika didn't give her friend a name. Usually, if you were talking about someone you knew well, you said their name, even if the person you were talking to didn't know them. There was also the sudden dilation of Erika's pupils, and the way she looked not at Lili, but at her shoulder. Clues.

Erika didn't want Lili knowing it was *her* book.

Molly's New Mom. Very interesting. Erika was looking for a woman's influence in her young life. That was natural when she was on the brink of womanhood. Still, she was keeping her wish a secret. Maybe the book hadn't found its way behind the couch accidentally at all, but rather it was a hiding place.

Behind them, the card game erupted as Linwood Daniels threw down his cards. "Dammit, Chester, you play cards like old people screw—not very well. We're gonna lose."

Lili glanced over as Roscoe narrowed his eyes to a beady stare just for Linwood.

"'Scuse me." Then Linwood raised his voice. "Sorry, Erika, that was very ungentlemanly of me with you present."

"It's all right, Mr. Daniels. I didn't even hear you."

Little fibber. Lili was sure she heard everything that went on. But it was sweet not to make the elderly man feel any worse.

Erika poked Lili's knee. "Are the cats talking yet?"

Lili glanced at Fluffy's high-rise fur coat. "No. I don't understand it." She understood perfectly: wounded male pride.

Einstein gagged as if she'd swallowed a hair ball.

"So maybe *you* should talk to Fluffy now."

What choice did she have with those beseeching blue eyes looking at her with such hope? While the child watched Fluffy for any signs, Lili closed her eyes.

Stop, you idiot human! A flashing red stoplight with a dunce cap on top of it. Einstein, giving her the evil green eye, understood the meaning of a promise. It shouldn't be broken, even if it was a human making it under duress.

Fake it. The accompanying image almost made her laugh: a woman on a bed, well, faking it for her lover. Where did Einstein come up with this stuff?

Lili cracked one eye open. Erika was watching with an intense blue gaze that seemed almost as soul-penetrating as Lady Dreadlock's. Lili couldn't feed her a pack of face-saving lies. "It's not working."

"But you said you can talk to animals." With a good, old-fashioned pout, Erika looked like the child she was.

"Sometimes they don't want to talk to me."

Erika tugged on a pigtail. "It's okay. I wasn't sure you could do it, anyway. Dad said—"

"I know what he said. Don't confuse efforts with results."

"I was expecting too much. You should never get your expectations out of whack with reality or you get crushed."

Good Lord, Tanner had taught the poor child that? "If you expect good things to happen, they usually do. But if you expect bad things to happen, well, then they do." Tanner was going to kill her for putting that thought into Erika's head.

"So then you're saying because I didn't really believe you could talk to Fluffy, that's why you can't?"

"Noo. That's not what I mean." God, she was making a muddle of this. "It wasn't meant to be right now. Sometimes that's the way things are. But that doesn't mean it won't work later." She couldn't stand letting Erika down this way.

"I like you anyway, Lili," Erika said as if she sensed Lili's distress. The child was extremely intuitive for her age.

Or maybe Lili had her misery written across her forehead. "Thank you, Erika. I like you, too." She patted the girl's knee. "Let's talk about something fun. What do you think of your dad's girlfriend?" Was she the woman Erika needed in her young life?

"He doesn't have a girlfriend."

"But you said he had a date." Lili didn't mention that she already knew about the date.

"She's not his girlfriend. It's just a date."

"But she could become something more." Lili was glad she'd made Tanner take the flowers. If she could get him to be more spontaneous on all levels, give him a little joie de vivre, there could be a wedding by June. Erika would have a kind-hearted mother who knew that effort was much more important than results.

Erika flapped her hand in typical childhood dismissal. "She can't be his girlfriend because he's never introduced me."

Lili felt her mouth drop open, but she couldn't seem to shut it again. Tanner hadn't brought his girlfriend home to meet his daughter? Then again, had he even said the woman was his girlfriend? Maybe they hadn't progressed that far.

"He doesn't want to introduce her to me."

Lili found her tongue. "Why ever not?"

"Well, some ladies aren't interested in being stepmoms. He probably hasn't even told her about me."

Where had the girl gotten an idea like that? Most likely from her friends at school. "You're his pride and joy. I don't believe he'd be able to stop talking about you."

Erika shrugged. "I can be kind of a know-it-all. He might be afraid I'd scare her away."

Tanner would dump a woman who didn't want to meet his daughter. Wouldn't he? Lili realized she didn't know Tanner all that well. "You're not a know-it-all."

"The kids at school think I am because I always raise my hand and I always get the answer right."

"That means you're smart, not a know-it-all." Oh, this poor child. "Your dad's terribly proud of you. I'm sure if he hasn't introduced you to this lady he's dating, he's got a good reason." Lili couldn't think of one right now.

Oh, my Lord, the poor child needed a mother badly. She needed someone to whom she could pour out her girlish troubles, someone to tell her she was sweet, smart and not a know-it-all. She'd probably never told Tanner what the other kids at school said. Worse, he might have poohpoohed it without realizing its effect on Erika. But a woman would have understood. There was something about girl-to-girl talk. Lili loved her Dad, but when she was growing up, it was her mom she'd told her troubles to.

A loud yelp and a high-pitched screech cut off all conversation. Dust bunnies flew behind the couch. Einstein was a streak of silver across the rag rug and out the door. At the pinochle table, Hiram Battle jerked out of his chair, knocked it over, and Fluffy, a marmalade flash in hot pursuit, barreled into his legs. The cat rolled and lay stunned for a long moment. Then he opened his yellow eyes, and shivers coursed his back.

"He's cracked his head on Hiram's shins," Chester said.

"More like the damn thing cracked *my* shins." Hiram bent down to rub both legs.

No one admonished him for the *damn*.

Fluffy leaped to his paws in a move only a dexterous feline could make, gave a shriek that shook the front window, then streaked out the door, his fur on end like an enraged porcupine, and disappeared up the stairs.

Linwood stared after him. "That cat's lost its marbles."

Hiram rubbed his shins once more for good measure. "It's a menace. What's wrong with it?"

Lili didn't know. Fluffy wasn't getting better. And her promise to Tanner was ripping her up.

CHAPTER SIX

SIPPING ON HER CAN OF cherry soda, Lili sat on her front porch, one leg dangling as she kept the swing chair in motion with her toes on the wood planks. The card game was still in full tilt next door, lights blazing in the ground-floor windows.

Lili contemplated the possibilities. Rita would be perfect for Chester Pawson, a movie star living right in his house. He'd adore Rita as much as he adored Deanna Durbin, except when the cat yowled. And Linwood Daniels would be perfect for Cy, short for Cyclops. Cy and Linwood had so much in common. The poor cat was a coyote war veteran. She'd lost an eye and half an ear to the battle, and her tail was bent at an odd angle, but she was tough. As for Hiram, Serenity? Hmm, maybe not. They'd probably kill each other. Lili had more thinking to do on that one.

Contemplating cat homes and that Erika needed a feminine influence was only part of the reason she was swinging on her front porch. She wanted to catch Tanner when he got home. First, there was no way someone in the house next door wouldn't mention her visit, so she had to head the argument off at the pass. Second, Einstein's presence had only infuriated Fluffy. And third, that body needed to be found. No two ways about it; Lili couldn't let Tanner play wait and see anymore.

He needed a push in the right direction.

Maybe Tanner hadn't introduced his daughter to the current woman in his life because it was only a physical thing. Just sex. If he was having *just* sex with his date, he'd be gone a good, long while. Unless he was a wham-bam-thank-you-ma'am type.

Eww. Really, she didn't want to think about Tanner having sex at all. It was one thing to send him off with flowers, quite another to imagine anything behind the bedroom door, at least if she wasn't the woman behind it with him.

You're hooked. Like a fish with the bait in its mouth.

Einstein was flumped between the tires of Lili's bike where it was padlocked to a porch rail, the only sign of life being the slight rise and fall of the cat's belly as she breathed. Her thoughts telegraphed right into Lili's brain.

"I am not hooked," Lili said aloud.

Then again, why did her heart suddenly start racing when a car pulled into *her* drive and Tanner got out?

His blue polo shirt hugged the contours of his chest and his blond hair picked up beams of moonlight falling through the trees as he traversed the stones to her front stoop, stepping from light to shadow and back again.

She waited until he'd climbed the two porch stairs. "How was your date?" She tried for enthusiasm and excitement.

He stuck his hands in the pockets of his Dockers. "Fine."

Fine? Gee, what woman would want to hear that? Lili

pushed off with her toes and set the swing once again into motion. "Did she like the flowers?"

"She thought they were fine."

"Fine?" This time she said the word aloud. The flowers were gorgeous. Even if she did say so herself.

He looked up, down, around, everywhere but at her.

And her stomach sank. "She hated them."

"No." He did the look-around thing again. "She thought they were extravagant, that I'd spent too much money on them."

"Oh." What kind of woman worried about a man being *too* extravagant? Erika needed a woman's influence in her life, but that didn't mean *this* one was the right woman.

Tanner rushed on to explain. "She's an accountant, you know, frugal by nature."

She made a little humphing noise. "I should have sent you down for carnations."

"It wouldn't have mattered. She isn't…like you."

Hmm. That was nice to hear. At least, she thought it was. Wasn't it? "Did *you* like them?" She held up a hand. "And don't use the word *fine*."

He smiled. Tanner had a nice smile that reached inside a girl and made her feel all tingly. "They were unique."

She dipped her head and looked at him through her lashes.

He rushed on to explain again. "Exotic? Perfect? Uniquely, perfectly, exotically you?"

It was a nice start. She wondered if the accountant's kisses were *fine*. Tanner needed more than that if he was going to find his joie de vivre. A new mother wouldn't do Erika any good if there wasn't a loving example to follow.

"Are you seeing her again?"

"You're a nosy little thing."

She jumped up from the swing and stepped up to him, rising to her full barefoot five feet eight inches. "Little?"

He smiled again.

Lili made up her mind. The frugal accountant wasn't right for Tanner. She wouldn't be right for Erika. "It's not my business, and I am nosy, but tell me anyway."

He gave her a long look she couldn't quite interpret, then his aura suddenly seemed to swirl with indigo, which she *could* interpret. She got a few of those tingles she'd felt when he'd pulled the stickers out of her hair.

"It's safe to say no," he murmured, "we're not compatible."

She was unprepared for how solidly the wave of relief swept through her and practically knocked her off her feet. "That's too bad. I'm sorry."

"Don't worry about it. I'm fine with the outcome."

There was that minimalist word again. She really, really wanted to know if his kisses would be more than fine. Purely from an experimental point of view. If Tanner was capable of more than fine, well, there was hope for him.

She stepped back, wrapping a hand around the porch post so she couldn't inadvertently wrap it around his very muscular arm or rest her fingers against his chest.

An image of that fish hook popped into her mind. Einstein, the beast, wore a snarky cat grin on her face. Cats did grin. You just had to know them well to figure out when they did it.

"I hope Erika won't be disappointed." Then she stopped. She didn't know how to bring up Erika's need

for a female influence without making it a slam against
Tanner's parenting skills. That would only put him on
the defensive; then he wouldn't listen to a single thing
she had to say.

He stuck his hands in his pockets. "Erika will be
fine, too."

He didn't say that was because Erika had never met
the woman in question, which would give Lili a lead-in
to talking about Erika's world view on know-it-alls and
the ladies Tanner dated.

Give it up. She might as well raise her hands in the
air in surrender, like the image Einstein sent her.

The cat was right. Lili didn't know if she should
open her big mouth and let it all out. She wasn't a parent,
after all. She didn't even have nieces or nephews. She
was much better at talking to animals. At least most of
the time, though she was definitely a miserable failure
with Fluffy. Come to think of it, she was a miserable
failure with the whole Rutland family.

Lili hugged the wood pillar of her porch. "I'm glad
she'll be *fine*," she said. "She seems like a resilient girl."

"She is."

"And I can see how proud of her you are."

Tanner smiled. "It shows that much?"

Lili beamed at him in return. "It shows."

Erika came first before everything, which was one of
the reasons he didn't introduce her to the women he
dated. Tanner didn't want Erika to become attached to
someone who would only be in their lives for a short
period of time. He didn't have any intention of remar-
rying, and it wouldn't be fair to have a woman enter
Erika's life only to leave a short time later.

Tanner's date with Anna hadn't been disastrous. They'd enjoyed a nice dinner at a wharf restaurant, then she'd simply given him the Dear John speech at her front door. Perhaps his male pride should have been wounded. Instead he'd only felt relief, primarily due to the fact that Lili had preoccupied his thoughts all evening.

Lili hugged the column tighter, as if she were dying to say something else, but couldn't get the words out. Tanner wouldn't have believed it if he wasn't witnessing it. Even she claimed she spoke before she thought.

"Spit it out, Lili."

She sighed. "Has Erika ever talked about having a new mom?"

He took a step backward and almost lost his footing down the first stair. "No."

"Oh. Well. Okay."

That definitely wasn't all Lili wanted to say on the subject. He just as definitely didn't want to hear it. Yet he felt compelled to go on. "We're fine the way we are."

"I'm sure you are." Oh, no, she wasn't sure, because she whispered, "It's that *word*."

"What word?"

"*Fine*. It's…" She let go of the porch column to swirl her hand in the air. "So average. Like when someone you've met once and haven't seen in a year politely asks how you've been and you say, 'Fine, thanks.' It's totally meaningless."

"It's a perfectly fine word."

She cocked her head at his sharp tone. "I'm not trying to offend you."

"I'm not offended." Actually, Lili made him feel a pang of guilt. *He* was fine, but had he ever stopped to ask Erika? Not that he'd marry to provide her with a new mother, but he had assumed she was as fine with their family situation as he was. "I've never thought about it before." Hell if that didn't make him feel like a bad father.

"I'm sorry. I won't say another word about it." Lili zipped her lip. "It's none of my business, anyway. It's not like I have kids or know the least little thing about how to raise them. Feel free to tell me to stop babbling. I told you I do that when I get nervous."

Actually, she did it most of the time, but that wasn't what had his gaze riveted to her pretty face. "I'm making you nervous right now?" He took back that step he'd put between them.

"Yes."

A one-word answer wasn't like the Lili he'd come to know…and semiappreciate. "Why?"

She had wide, beautiful eyes even in the dim porch lighting.

"Because…" She bit her lip, something that at this moment he found extremely enticing.

He took one more step, closer, very close. "Spit it out, Lili," he whispered. "I won't bite." Well, only under certain circumstances. And he'd make sure she liked it.

"Okay, here's the thing."

He had a feeling he wasn't going to like what she had to say. Having known her all of twenty-four hours, he'd already learned she prefaced an unpalatable notion with that statement.

"I know you told me I couldn't tell Erika or Roscoe about Fluffy seeing the murder—" she held up her palm as if she had her other hand on a Bible "—and I swear I didn't. But I did go over to visit." She took a deep breath, then rushed on. "To see how Fluffy was doing, but I didn't talk to him. I was hoping he'd be better, but he wasn't."

Did she think he was such an ogre that he'd get angry because she'd gone to his house for a visit? Tanner mentally shrugged. Hell, he had issued a lot of edicts, so no wonder she thought he was the ogre.

"It's fine, Lili—" Then he stopped himself. She didn't like that word. "It doesn't bother me that you went over to my house, and I appreciate your concern for Fluffy, and thank you for not saying anything about a murder."

"I asked Einstein to talk to him. You didn't specifically say Einstein couldn't talk to him, only that I couldn't."

He almost put his face in his hands to stifle the laughter, but Lili seemed so concerned. As if she thought she'd committed some cardinal sin. "What did Fluffy and Einstein talk about?"

She huffed out a great puff of air and turned to look at the lump lying by the bike tires. Tanner had thought it was a pillow, but now he noticed the green stare trained right on him.

"Not a thing. Einstein doesn't make friends well."

"Then how does Einstein get along with Wanetta's cats?"

"They let her be the leader."

A womanly attribute. Tanner had the sense not to say that.

Lili peeled herself away from the porch pillar, leaned close enough for him to smell something sweet and heady, something all woman, something he wanted, and put her hand on his upper arm.

"I need to help Fluffy." She looked up at him with an earnest gaze, her lips parted, her eyes deep in the shadow.

On someone else, it might have been beguiling, manipulative even, but with Lili, it was simply sincere.

"You want me to help you find that body," he said for her.

"Yes." She punctuated with a nod, her dark hair falling like a curtain over one shoulder.

What did she get out of claiming Fluffy saw a murder? What emotional need did it fill for her? Despite his speech about not being one hundred percent sure she couldn't talk to animals, he hung on to that ninety-nine percent certainty. That meant she had to get some emotional charge out of the assertion.

What the hell did it matter? If he gave in and went with her, they wouldn't find a body, but she would have to give up this nonsense. "I'll take you."

She simply stared at him. Her breath puffed in the open collar of his shirt and right down beneath his belt buckle.

Lili could never remain speechless for long. "You're kidding, right? I mean, you'll pack up and move away during the night, or you'll call the men in white with the straitjacket."

"I won't move away, and I don't think they use straitjackets anymore. When I say I'm going to do something, I do it."

She smiled. It almost stopped his heart. Then she threw her arms around his neck, stepping on his shoe as she went up on her tiptoes to hug him. Her hair caressed his face. Her small, firm breasts pressed to his chest. She was plastered against him yet he wanted her closer. Slipping his arms around her waist, he made sure she couldn't let go.

"Thank you, thank you, thank you." She kissed his ear, his cheek, warm, moist kisses that weakened his knees.

His brain short-circuited, and his body went into overdrive. He pulled back, grabbed her face in his hands and took her lips openmouthed. She responded with a low sound, a moan not much louder than a hitch of breath, but it was enough to make him want to push her to the wooden porch. She let him take her with hungry kisses, her tongue in his mouth, his in hers, a tender nip of her lip, then a soul-deep mating. Over and over until she was once again plastered to him, and the hard ridge of his erection burned against her belly. She tasted of cherry soda and sizzled like champagne. She melted into him and turned him inside out.

He had never tasted anything like her, never touched anything as soft, never wanted anything as badly.

He was on her front porch. Next door to his front porch. With gaps between the hedge that anyone could see through.

As much as he wanted to take more, Tanner pulled back.

His lips clamored for another taste. His cock ached to be inside her. Hell, he simply vibrated all over with want of her.

She slid down his body until her feet were back on the porch and opened her eyes. "Wow."

That was putting it mildly. He'd have said that, if he were capable of speech. She kept her arms looped around his neck, supporting herself against him as if her legs wouldn't hold her. He wasn't sure his could hold him for much longer.

"That was a very *fine* kiss."

He laughed, though it came out sounding a bit strangled. It was a damn sight more than fine, and he was truly beginning to understand her earlier analogy.

"I think I might dream about it tonight," she said with a little smile and her eyelids at half mast.

He would be dreaming about far more than just that kiss.

Sliding her arms down his chest, she put her hands flat against him and pushed away until she touched him with nothing but the tips of her fingers.

"Cat got your tongue?" she said.

No. Lili did. He realized he had to say something or he'd look like a besotted idiot. "What time shall we go tomorrow?"

She gave a happy little sigh, took another step back, breaking all physical contact. "I have to work until noon. Then it takes me half an hour to ride home."

He had to resist the urge to pull her back into his arms. "Do you want me to pick you up?"

"No, thanks. I like the ride."

He dropped down to the first porch stair. "Then I'll see you at twelve-thirty."

With another step, he was on the path and heading for home. The distance, and the fact that her scent didn't cloud his mind anymore, gave him back a semblance of perspective.

A burst of laughter erupted on his front porch, followed by the gravel pitch of male voices. Roscoe's pinochle buddies. The game must be breaking up. He hadn't a clue how he'd explain tomorrow's trek with Lili to Roscoe and Erika, but at least once it was over, life could return to normal.

Except for a kiss that would haunt him and a woman who would follow him into his dreams.

"Tanner?"

He turned.

"What's your date's name?"

He looked at her, cocking his head to the side. "I can't remember." It was true for a few moments. In fact, for that same amount of time, he couldn't even picture her face.

Lili smiled, the slightest curve of her lips. "Then I guess you are fine about the relationship being over."

"More than fine, Lili."

He was fine about not seeing Anna anymore. He wasn't sure how fine he was going to be now that he'd tasted Lili. He had a feeling that one sip of her sweet lips wasn't going to be enough.

CHAPTER SEVEN

"HELL'S BELLS, YOU SEDUCED HIM! I was joking, Lili." Kate pushed her tumbling hair back. It wouldn't stay no matter what she did. Maybe it was time to chop the whole mess off.

"I did not seduce him. He said he'd take me to look for the body before I kissed him." Lili tipped her head in typical Lili fashion as she tinkered with one of her unusual flower creations. "Actually, I think he kissed me first. I only kissed him back."

"You don't know for sure who was the kisser and who was the kissee?" If Kate didn't know better, she'd think Lili was a total ditz. However, Lili wasn't ditzy so much as...uncomplicated.

Kate flipped open her calendar on the counter to make sure her appointments for the day were in line. Saturday mornings were slow for walk-ins but busy in the back room where the arranging was done. Kate had just returned from delivering wedding flowers. The bride was a mess, but the bouquets Sasha, her best designer, had made were gorgeous. This afternoon she had a funeral to see to. But for now, the shop front was devoid of customers and offered the perfect backdrop for a heart-to-heart. Sometimes Kate felt like Lili's older sister. She was more than a boss; she considered herself Lili's friend.

Lili clipped off a wilted bloom. "Now that I think about it, he definitely kissed me first. After I hugged him profusely for agreeing to take me into the woods."

"I think he has other things on his mind besides looking for a body." Unless he was looking for *Lili's* body. That might be a good thing. Lili needed someone to give her life direction, and this Tanner guy sounded practical. As well as hot.

"I'm only concerned about helping Fluffy and Erika and finding that body Fluffy saw."

Right. That was why her flower creation was suddenly so engrossing. "How well does he kiss?"

"Kate! That's personal!"

"Since when have you held back personal stuff?" Interesting. There was more than just a kiss going on here.

"It was fine." For some odd reason, Lili winced, then she shrugged and went on. "It was a good kiss, but now that Tanner's going to help me, I don't need to kiss him again."

"Maybe you don't *need* to, but do you *want* to?"

The overhead bell on the front door tinkled, and Lili was saved from answering. For now. Kate wasn't going to drop the issue, however.

"Hi, Mr. Swann," Lili said brightly, as if she thought she'd been saved from the conversation for all time.

He looked dapper in a pinstripe suit, charcoal shirt and silver tie. He was delicious, Kate had to admit that much. But what on earth was he doing here? As if she didn't know.

Lili stared all googly-eyed as only Lili could manage

without looking silly. Then she grabbed the watering can and headed for the philodendrons in the front window. The philodendrons Lili had watered when she'd arrived this morning.

Joe dropped an envelope on the counter. "I was driving by so I thought I'd drop off your check."

"That's so kind of you." Kate liked punctual customers, but his visit had nothing to do with timely payment. "You didn't have to go out of your way. Next time, put it in the mail." She said it as sweetly as possible, but the message was there.

Before she knew it, he'd reached over the counter and smoothed several strands of her falling hairdo back off her ear. The touch was warm, almost sensual, and her whole body reacted with a wave of heat that thankfully didn't make it to her cheeks. Thank God she hadn't taken off her suit jacket or he would have seen the purely involuntary peak of her nipples.

"What—" her teeth clamped down on the end of the word "—are you doing?"

"Stealing an opportunity to touch you." Then he smiled. Mercy, he had a smile. He also disarmed her pithy comebacks by stating his intentions flat out.

"Mr. Swann—"

"Joe to you."

"Didn't we do this routine yesterday?"

"No. I've got a different routine today. Everything on schedule for this afternoon?"

He changed the subject so abruptly he left her wondering what today's routine actually was.

"Sasha's finishing up." She glanced at her watch. "Oscar will deliver to the church in an hour and to the site by one." She omitted saying the word *cemetery*. She wasn't afraid of dying as Joe had intimated yesterday, but she got a peculiar stomach roll, and she didn't need a psychiatrist to tell her why. When her mother had found out she had cancer, she'd insisted they make the funeral arrangements. It was cheaper to do it *before* you needed them. Mom had been a planner. But at the age of twenty-one, with her mom's inevitable death clearly on the horizon, funeral arrangements had been the last thing Kate could handle.

Kate shook off the unsettling memories. "How is Mrs. Minnick?"

Mr. Minnick had keeled over on their neighbor's driveway while out for his morning jog. Heart attack. He was fifty-five.

"As well as can be expected." The color of Joe's eyes deepened to the lapis shade Lili had earlier admired. While he was witty and charming and could coax a laugh or a tingle out of Kate when she tried her best to remain immune, he also felt deeply for the families he worked with. His compassion wasn't faked.

She felt herself being sucked into his gaze. "Would you like to see the progress?" At least she wouldn't be semialone with him. The back room was a beehive of activity right now.

"I trust your judgment. Are you busy tomorrow afternoon?"

"Why?" It was rude, but he'd already said he had another routine in mind. She saw it coming a mile away.

"My brother's new baby will be christened in the morning, and we're having a barbecue afterward. I'd like you to come."

Other than weddings and funerals, she didn't attend church. Her mother hadn't brought her up that way. Plus, a christening was so family oriented. She didn't do family barbecues, either.

She raised one eyebrow. "Do you want a polite excuse or a flat no?"

"How about a 'Yes, Joe, I'd love to meet your family and spend the afternoon with you'?"

"*Mr.* Swann, we went over this yesterday."

"And I clearly stated I wasn't going to give up."

She gave a half snort, half laugh. "So you thought I'd be more likely to agree to a christening than a lunch date?"

He smiled, and an endearing dimple she'd never noticed before appeared by the side of his mouth. "It was worth a shot."

She was flattered. Mercy, she was even tempted when he smiled like that, but the harder he pushed, the more she knew he was a man to steer clear of. Hadn't he mentioned nesting and babies yesterday? If anyone's biological clock was ticking, it was his. It had probably hit overtime when his brother had had a child.

"The shot missed its mark," she quipped.

"Then we'll skip the christening and do the barbecue." He waggled an eyebrow. "My nephew is adorable."

This time she outright laughed. He did so amuse her with his persistence. "No, Joe. And no means no this time. Just like last time."

He looked at her, a slight curve to his mouth, the dimple extinguished. Then he stroked a finger along the line of her jaw, shooting another tingle straight to her unruly nipples. "You called me Joe. See, that wasn't so hard."

"You know, some women could mistake you for a

stalker. You're *annoyingly* persistent," she added with a smile.

He held her gaze a moment, then, both hands on the counter, he leaned in until his lips were next to her ear and whispered, "If I'm annoying you, why are your nipples hard enough to show right through that lovely tailored jacket you're wearing?"

Damn. With his warm breath against her ear, her nipples started to ache. "I'm cold."

"Actually, I think you're hot. Very hot. In more ways than one." He pulled back, a gleam in his eye. Then he saluted her. "Until our next skirmish."

The problem was Kate looked forward to the next skirmish. She looked forward to seeing him. Before you knew it, she might even accept one of his offers. For sex. *Only* for sex. He'd lit a fire in her with today's routine and putting it out herself wasn't going to work to her satisfaction.

KATE LOOKED UP AT THE TINKLE of the overhead bell. "Thank God he's gone."

"Joe asked you out?" Lili was fairly jumping inside.

"Don't tell me," Kate said, ticking off something on her calendar, "that you weren't straining with every fiber of your being to hear what we were discussing."

Lili abandoned the empty watering can by the side of the smaller refrigerator unit. "I was straining *not* to listen."

"Well, he's gone. So let's get back to our original discussion. You and Tanner Rutland. Is there a spark there?"

"The kiss was an *experiment,* Kate. I wanted to see if he was capable of joie de vivre." Though she hadn't expected it to be bone-melting. It was *just* a kiss.

"But *he* kissed you first. After you hugged *him* profusely."

Kate never forgot a *thing*. "I thought we were done with that conversation." Lili put her elbows on the counter and propped her chin on her palms. "I'd much rather hear about whether you're going out with Joe."

"Mr. Swann to you. And I'm not dating him." Kate wore a militant glare that was highly unusual for her. Joe must have pushed one of her buttons and pushed it hard.

"Why not? The real reason, not the one about how he works with dead people. He works with the grieving, not the dead."

Kate looked at Lili as if she'd never seen her before. Or she'd sprouted horns. "That's what *he* said."

"I think it's noble."

Kate nodded, her gaze faraway for a fraction of a second. Then she was back. "He's looking for a relationship, maybe even marriage." She made a face as if even the word were distasteful. "And I'm not. Flowers By Nature is my life and growing it is my goal. I don't have time for anything else."

Lili swayed on her elbows, her chin resting in her hands. "I don't see why you can't have a relationship *and* Flowers By Nature."

"Marriage and relationships aren't part of my life plan."

Lili knew that. She even admired Kate's tenacity. But she wondered also if Kate would be lonely somewhere down the road. Even Kate's mother had succumbed to instinct and had had a child in her late thirties. Lili knew the whole story. Kate's mom had wanted a child, but she hadn't wanted a husband. As far as "Mom" was concerned, men were just sperm donors.

Kate didn't even know who the man was. The weird thing was that didn't seem to bother Kate, that her father was just a *sperm*.

"I've forgotten why the plan is so important." Lili hadn't grasped the concept. Not having a plan seemed more spontaneous and given to encouraging joie de vivre. Which made her think of Tanner. Was her kiss better than his date's kiss? Was it better than fine? God, she shouldn't think about that.

"If you don't have a plan, you end up reacting to things rather than taking action. Things happen *to* you instead of *you* making things happen the way you want." Then Kate centered her tenacious focus on Lili. "What about you? Don't you want to get married and have children?"

Lili played her fingers on her lips. "Someday."

"When?" Tenacious Kate was on a roll.

She shrugged. "I haven't planned it out to the nth degree."

"You're thirty-one. You should start planning for it."

Leaning over the counter like that, her back had begun to ache and Lili straightened. "It'll happen when it's right."

"But you don't even date."

"I do too."

"When was your last date?"

Lili had to think hard. "Last year."

She'd dated Dirk three times when she'd very gently spoken to his parrot about the problem of tearing out its neck feathers. Dirk had gone gaga. He'd started having parties where she was the star attraction. Like a circus freak. Before that, Norton had lasted four dates. She'd told him his puppy was chewing the sofa because he was lonely when Norton was at work. The next thing Lili knew, he'd locked the poor dog in the bathroom so she couldn't contaminate him. They were back-to-back examples of the either-or theory. Men either became obsessed or they freaked.

She was sure Tanner wasn't going to be any different.

"If you want to have a family, you need to start planning now. Or suddenly you'll be forty, unmarried and childless."

"Women can have children after forty." She'd like to be a mother. But she wouldn't mind being a stepmother, either. She wasn't like the ladies Erika had referred to.

"That's not my point."

"I get the point. I don't *make* life happen, I let it happen *to* me. But I like the unexpected, and the unexpected doesn't happen when you plan for it. Then you just get the expected."

Kate sighed. "I don't know how, but in an extremely complicated manner, you make the illogical sound logical."

"My dad says that, too." Lili smiled. "It's a compliment."

Kate threw up her hands. "Whatever. We'll have to agree to disagree on this one."

"How about I agree to make one plan? Will that make you feel better?"

"I shudder to think what that plan might be." Kate did just that, shuddered, and her topknot fell off her head.

"Okay, I'm making my plan." Lili closed her eyes as if she were wishing on a star or blowing out birthday candles.

She made a plan to take the bull by the horns and tell Tanner that his daughter was pining for a mother.

That meant she had two plans, because this afternoon, she was going to solve the mystery of Fluffy's communiqué.

Wow, this whole plan-making thing wasn't so bad.

TANNER COULDN'T STAND SEEING Erika like this. He was well aware she knew how to turn on the watering pot when she wanted something, but the tears coursing down her cheeks this morning were not the fake variety. She hadn't touched the pancakes Roscoe had made. She hadn't even poured her syrup.

"Daddy, he's getting worse all the time." She only called him *Daddy* when she was truly upset. "Look at him."

All Tanner could see was Fluffy's nose sticking out from between the kitchen cabinet and the stove. Somehow, the cat had squeezed into a space that was half its body girth. Fluffy had been under Erika's bed when Tanner had gotten home last night. This morning, when he'd tried to put it outside, the cat had left a scratch along his forearm, then wedged itself into the small cavity between stove and cupboard.

"Lili says she can't help him if he won't talk to her. She's nice, but I don't think she can talk to animals, anyway." Erika's attitude had soured as Fluffy's condition deteriorated. Last night, she'd been willing to give Lili the benefit of the doubt. This morning, she no longer believed.

He felt a bottomless well of guilt inside, and the pancakes he'd eaten sat like rocks in the pit of his stomach. Christ, he wanted his little girl to grow up with a practical head on her shoulders, but the anguish on her pretty face tore his guts out.

"Honey, you're not eating your pancakes." Roscoe set his own plate down on the tablecloth and poured a dollop of syrup, then upended the bottle on Erika's pancakes.

"I'm not hungry, Grandpa."

"Well, wipe your tears, honey. We'll take Fluffy back over to see Lili. I'm sure it'll work this time."

It wouldn't work because Tanner had refused to let Lili talk to Fluffy. She might try every trick in the book to get around the promise while sticking to the letter of it, but she wouldn't outright talk to the cat when he'd told her not to.

"Eat your breakfast, sweetheart," he murmured.

Erika gave him a woeful look, but she ate. Slowly. Each mouthful a reluctant acquiescence to his command.

Tanner pondered the issues. If he shielded Erika too much, she'd never learn to make her own choices and decisions. In Lili's case, was he forcing his own closed-mindedness on his daughter? As a parent, it was his responsibility to make decisions that were in her best interests, but it was also his duty to let her make some of those choices herself. It was a wise man who knew which decisions to turn over to her.

How wise are you, Tanner?

Not very. Hell, he knew where his closed-mindedness came from. His own bad memories. He'd loved Erika's mother, but he hadn't liked a lot of her wacky ideas. He closed his eyes. He hadn't thought about that last fight between them in so long it had almost faded from his memory. Until Lili had brought it back last night. Karen had believed she had powerful latent psychic abilities, and she'd wanted to go on a retreat to unlock her powers. A six-week-long retreat in Sedona.

It was the last in a long line of arguments. He'd refused. Erika had been only two; he couldn't let Karen leave for six weeks. To him, it was tantamount to abandoning her child.

She'd gone anyway, while he'd been at work, leaving Erika with Wanetta next door. And a note for him saying she'd be back. She hadn't come back. She'd died in a car accident on her way to Sedona, and he swore he'd never tell a living soul that she'd left Erika like that. He also swore he'd give his daughter the sort of practical mind her mother hadn't had.

But had he gone too far? He'd never considered re-marriage, never even considered what living with two men would be like for Erika. Since his own mother had passed long before Erika was born, if it hadn't been for Wanetta living next door, Erika wouldn't have had a single female inspiration in her life. Had he robbed his daughter of something precious?

"I'll go with you," he said as if several minutes hadn't elapsed since Roscoe's offer to take Fluffy next door. "But Lili's at work right now, so it'll have to be after lunch."

Roscoe raised a brow that definitely asked, "How the hell do you know where Lili is?"

Tanner answered as if Roscoe had spoken aloud. "I saw her last night when I got home. She mentioned her visit." He looked from his father to his daughter. "She told me what's wrong with Fluffy."

"But she said she didn't know, Dad." At least he was back to being *Dad*.

"I asked her not to tell you."

"Why?" The look his daughter leveled on him was a

mixture of horror and disbelief, as if he'd somehow betrayed her.

The wound cut deep. In protecting her, he hadn't trusted her judgment. It was as simple as that. He wanted to teach her practicality. Instead, he'd stolen the opportunity for her to make up her own mind about Lili's abilities. There came a time where the explanation couldn't be simply because he said so. "I deemed it inappropriate for someone your age. However, I've reconsidered my initial evaluation and revised my opinion."

"What did Lili say?" Even Roscoe gave him the evil eye.

In his gut, Tanner didn't want Erika involved, but *involved* was a relative term. He didn't plan to take her along while searching for the body, but his daughter stood to learn two lessons. First, there were all kinds of people out there, some honest, some charlatans, some out of their minds. She'd have to learn to tell the difference. If Lili, by some weird cosmic chance, was right, Erika needed to learn that there was evil in the world, sometimes close to home. Only then would she know how to protect herself from it. The best thing he could do was provide her with adequate tools to make those determinations.

Tanner rose and carried his empty plate to the sink, then he turned, resting his hands on the counter behind him. "Lili believes Fluffy saw a murder. A real murder of a human being. She'd like my help in searching for the body." He eyed Erika. "Do you think she could be right or that she's definitely wrong?" Or something in between. "And what should we do about it?"

"I know what we should do."

Tanner held up his hand. "I'm not asking you, Roscoe. I'm asking Erika."

His daughter doodled her fork in the syrup swimming on her plate. "Well." She sucked her lower lip between her teeth. "It's like the missing link, Dad. Nobody's seen it, but that doesn't mean it isn't out there waiting to be found. Lots of really smart people believe in it."

Damn. She amazed him yet again. He'd given up that dream of being a great anthropologist as childish folderol, yet she'd made a connection he hadn't considered.

With the resilience of youth, she brightened right before his eyes. "It'll be like a controlled experiment. If we find it, Lili's psychic. If we don't, then she's not. It doesn't make her a bad person."

"I've never thought Lili is a bad person."

"But do you believe her?"

He wanted Erika to have her own opinion, even if it differed with his. "I'm inclined to think she might be wrong about this. But you need to decide for yourself."

She pressed her lips together in thought, then nodded. "You've always taught me to question things before making up my mind, so why not question that maybe Lily's right instead of questioning that maybe she's wrong?"

He'd taught her that? Hell, maybe he wasn't doing as bad a job at raising her as he'd suddenly begun to suspect.

He pulled out the chair, facing it toward her, and sat. "But if there is a body, do you understand what that means?"

She gave him a look. *Well, duh, Dad.* "It means that there *is* a very bad person who did a terrible thing."

"It also means it's not a game. It's very serious."

"That's why it's our duty to help Lili. Just in case."

She was so damn logical, the way he wanted her to be. But if there was a body, what the hell would he do then?

He leaned his elbows on his knees, laced his hands and pointed his index fingers at Erika. "There is no 'we' about it. You're not going with us."

"Aw, Dad, come on."

"No."

"Why not?"

"Because I said so." Sometimes that *was* all a parent needed to say.

ROSCOE SMILED. HE COULDN'T have finagled that one better if he'd done it himself. A whole afternoon, just the two of them. He'd packed a nice lunch and some cold drinks for them.

"I don't see why I can't go," Erika said as Tanner waved one last time before disappearing into the woods with Lili.

"Your dad's right, honey, this expedition isn't any place for you." Not that Roscoe expected them to find a body.

Lili, as magical and sweet as she was, had gotten her wires crossed on that one. Still, he had high hopes Lili could show Tanner a thing or two. She'd already gotten him to open up enough to allow the possibility that there were other ways of viewing the world besides only the practical one.

"Grandpa, do you think Fluffy saw a murder?"

He glanced at her as she shaded her eyes for a last longing look into the woods. "I hope not."

"Me, too. I like Lili and everything, but I hope she fails the controlled experiment." Then she looked up at him. "Grandpa, do you think Dad will ever want to get remarried?"

Heh. Great minds thought alike.

"Well, I don't know, honey, not for sure." He squeezed her hand. "But we can hope. We can surely hope."

CHAPTER EIGHT

"HOW FAR DO WE NEED TO GO?" Tanner tossed over his shoulder.

"I'm not sure," Lili admitted. "Cats *can* go for miles and miles. Or they can stick pretty close to home. Depends."

Tanner had donned hiking boots, jeans and a long-sleeved rugby shirt that did very nice things for his chest. The teal and green stripes set off his eye color nicely, bringing out a slightly turquoise hue. The sun on his hair was glaringly bright as he stepped between the shadows and light falling through the trees. But walking behind him was proving to be the biggest distraction of all. Lili had a hard time focusing on anything but his rear in the tight jeans.

She supposed she should do a lot less checking out of Tanner's butt and be a lot more worried about looking for the body. But somehow "the body" seemed more like a concept than a real human being. Or maybe thinking of it that way made everything easier for her. Sometimes delusion was a good thing.

"What exactly does it depend on?" Tanner asked.

The pack filled with Roscoe's sandwiches and sodas bobbed on his back. He had a strong stride, but Lili was long-legged and in the five or so minutes they'd been walking, keeping up hadn't proven to be a problem. Especially since she liked the view. Another five and they'd reach the meadow.

"Depends on how close they want to stay to the available food supply." She zipped her jacket. The sun's heat hadn't reached the shade. Spring in the mountains, while gorgeous, could be several degrees cooler than over in Silicon Valley.

"Then I'm surprised Fluffy wandered off at all." Talking didn't make Tanner lose his stride one bit.

"That's what Einstein said." Einstein had scampered ahead on the trail, darting in and out of the trees' shadows and sticking her paw down a few gopher holes without much success.

Lili couldn't quite believe Tanner had told Erika and Roscoe what the cat had seen. See, that was how the world worked. She'd made a decision to act, and everything suddenly went her way, as if *deciding* to do something made it happen. She knew that didn't mean Tanner believed in her ability, but it was one step closer to…well, not total acceptance, but closer to the possibility that the impossible *might* be possible.

She'd wanted to have a talk with Fluffy before they left, but the cat was having none of that. He'd been squished between a cabinet and the stove all morning, and he wasn't coming out for anything. So they were walking blind. All Lili had was the image of the oak tree and the forest surrounding the meadow. But which out of all these trees was the right tree?

"When did you first start talking to animals?"

She figured that question came because she'd nonchalantly mentioned Einstein. "I was seven. At least, that was the first time I realized not everyone talked to animals."

"Tell me about it."

She was sure Tanner didn't really want to know, but she'd lull him with a story or two, then launch into Erika's problem. It was a great plan. Kate would be proud of her. "My gerbil ate her babies. They were there in the morning, then three were missing in the afternoon. When I said that was a terrible thing to do, she told me to mind my own business."

He stopped so quickly she almost ran into his back. Or rather the pack on his back. He stood stock still for two seconds, then turned. Even in her hiking boots, she had to look up to meet his eyes.

"You're kidding, right?"

"I would never kid about my gerbil eating her babies. It was potentially traumatizing at my tender age. But I got over it when I realized it was in the natural order of things."

"Like Bigfoot having you for dinner?"

"Yeah." Tanner was like Kate. He didn't forget even a minor thing she'd said two days ago. "Gerbils eat their babies all the time. So do hamsters."

"So how'd you handle your little cannibal?"

"Once I figured out her natural tendencies, I put her babies in a separate cage."

He shook his head. "All I can say is I'm glad I never got Erika a gerbil." Then he started off again along the path, lobbing the next question over his shoulder. "What did your parents think of all this?"

"At first they thought I had a great imagination and went off on a tangent about how I'd be some great Nobel Prize-winning author someday. So they were very dis-

appointed when I decided I didn't want to go to college."
She looked sternly at his back. "Do you think everyone
has to go to college?"

He'd gone several strides before he finally said, "Not
necessarily. But it does help a person get ahead in life."

She figured he'd taken so long to answer because he
didn't want to offend her. "But if a person doesn't 'get
ahead,' does that necessarily mean one is actually behind?"

He sighed deeply. "I've never thought about it. Don't
you have plans for your future?"

That was what Kate wanted to know. "I think
planning for the future gets in the way of living the
present. And I'm not sure it makes a person happier or
less stressed out."

He didn't say anything, and she realized *she* might
have offended *him*. Obviously he was a planner, and he
might infer that she was saying he was unhappy and
stressed out. Or that he'd made Erika that way. "Not
everyone has to think the way I do. You have to plan
because you've got a child to consider. It's about taking
care of Erika."

Now that was a jolly good lead-in to what she'd
wanted to discuss anyway. "Okay, here's the thing."

This time he stopped and turned all in one movement.
"Do you realize you always preface something you
think I'm not going to like with that phrase?"

"Is that a bad thing?"

He cocked his head, then a smile grew on his
handsome face. "Probably not. At least I'm warned."

Lili smiled back. "So do you want to hear it or not?"

Tanner tipped his head back and looked at the sky
through the trees for a long moment. The sky was the

bright blue of a jaybird's wings, and clouds drifted lazily toward the sun.

Then he dropped his gaze to hers. She'd been waiting expectantly, an odd tension riding her shoulders as if she thought he'd shoot her down. The smallest of breezes picked up several strands of her dark hair and blew them across her lips, then seemed to spiral down and flirt with the hem of her skirt.

She didn't believe in planning her future, but she had faced down a cannibalistic gerbil when she was seven years old. He was sure, if he analyzed the tale, there'd be a moral message, something beyond that mothers shouldn't eat their children. Lili had a way of making him think about things in a different light. A fresh, unique perspective, even if it was totally alien to him.

"Yes, I'd like to hear what you're burning to tell me."

She squared her shoulders then wiggled her arms like a prizefighter getting ready for a bout. "Remember yesterday when we were talking about you no longer seeing the woman you'd been dating, and I asked if Erika was okay with that and you said she was fine and she never thought about having a new mom?"

That one took a bit of mulling over to get the whole gist. "Yeah, I do." That had been about the time he'd kissed her. Which explained why he didn't remember it all that clearly.

"I asked about that for a very specific reason."

He resisted telling her to get to the point. She'd get there when she was ready and not a moment before.

"Erika thinks you don't introduce her to your girl-friends because a) they aren't interested in being stepmoms, b) you're afraid to tell them about her, and/or

c) they're going to think she's a know-it-all and dump you." She let out a big breath when she was done, deflating like the air out of a balloon.

He jiggled his head to make sure it was attached. "My daughter said all that?"

She huffed and rolled her eyes. "Those were the things I boiled it down to."

He didn't know what to tackle first. "I don't have a girlfriend. I have never had a girlfriend. I just…go on dates sometimes. There isn't any point in introducing her."

What was he supposed to say to Erika about that? "They're not my girlfriends, sweetheart, I just have casual sex with them when I get horny because that's what men do." Holy hell, no.

Lili looked at him. If he'd been wearing a tie, or a dress shirt with a collar, he'd be running his finger around his neck trying to loosen it. She didn't ask, but he knew she knew exactly what he was thinking.

"*If* I ever meet a woman I'm serious about—"

"And so far, they've only been *fine*."

He clenched his teeth. "I will introduce Erika. I'm not ashamed of her."

He wasn't embarrassed about having needs, nor of taking care of those needs in an uncomplicated fashion. He was, however, ashamed he hadn't paid attention to what Erika needed. He didn't know how the hell to provide whatever "it" was, but he should have seen there was a problem.

"What's this know-it-all business? I've never told her that. She's everything I want my little girl to be."

"The kids at school call her that."

"I'll talk to her teachers."

"Do you know she has a book called *Molly's New Mom?* I think that's what she wants."

He'd never thought of himself as a bad father, but within two days, Lili had somehow managed to make him doubt everything he'd done with his daughter. He shoved his hands through his hair. "I can't get married because it's what Erika wants."

Lili pressed her lips together. "I suppose not." She tipped her head and blinked her lush lashes.

He had to stop thinking about her eyelashes. "I don't think I understood the impact losing Wanetta had on her."

Lili smiled, a fond, faraway smile. "Wanetta adored her."

"I'll have to find her another Wanetta. She's around me and old men too much."

"I'm not trying to say you're a bad father, Tanner. In fact, you're the best father I've ever known."

"And how many have you known?"

She looked over his left shoulder, then his right. "Not a lot." She shook her finger at him. "But I can still see how great you are and how much you love Erika and she loves you."

"But you think she needs something more."

"More? I don't know. Maybe for you to tell her why you haven't introduced her to your girlfriends."

"I told you they aren't my girlfriends," he said and immediately wished the words back. He did not want to say that sometimes he was a randy thirty-seven-year-old male who wanted to come inside a woman instead of in his own hand.

The truth was, he'd lain awake most of last night thinking about coming inside Lili. Over and over.

He'd fantasized about kissing her, about taking her with his mouth.

"You're looking at me funny."

"I'm not looking at you funny." He was looking at her as if he wanted to do all of those things right now. *As if.* There was no *as if* about it.

"We'd better get going," she said. "We've got a body to find. And thank you for telling Erika and Roscoe the truth."

He wasn't going to tell her his decision had more to do with Erika than his own thoughts on the subject. But she was right; they'd better get going before he didn't let her go at all.

"I'M THIRSTY." LILI WAS FEELING defeated. Her spirits had begun high, but they'd circled the meadow twice in an hour and hadn't found a thing. Out in the sun, away from the trees, it was hot. The tips of the long grasses swayed gently, but she could barely feel the breeze on her face and the sun baked the top of her head. A crow took flight from the top of a huge oak—not the oak she was looking for; they'd already checked—and the distant chatter of agitated squirrels echoed through the field.

"You want a sandwich?" Tanner stripped off the backpack.

The sight made her tipsy, his chest rippling as he used both hands to peel off the straps.

Their earlier conversation wasn't over. She'd gotten him to *think* about what Erika needed, but she wanted to provide a solution. That would take more thinking.

Tanner handed her one of the tuna sandwiches and a can of soda. She popped the top and drained it in three big slugs. It was unladylike, but she was parched. Einstein bounded over as soon as she'd flopped down in the long meadow grass and opened the plastic sandwich Baggie. Lili pulled out a chunk of tuna salad and fed it to her. Einstein didn't thank her. That was one thing TV hadn't taught her.

"Why can't the cat follow its nose and find what we're looking for?" Knee up, one leg crossed over the other ankle, Tanner made quick work of the sandwich.

Probably because she was too busy chasing gophers. It was the challenge of catching them that fascinated Einstein. They could pop back into their holes so quickly.

"I don't know." She put her face down low to Einstein's. "If she were a *good* cat, she'd have found it days ago."

If you weren't an idiot human, you wouldn't be asking a cat to do a human's job. Talk about a convoluted set of images; Einstein took the cake, but Lili got the insult.

Tanner finished his soda. For some reason, watching him in the simple act of drinking made Lili warm all over. He'd looked at her funny earlier, with an odd, burning intensity that made her feel as if he'd stripped her clothes off and licked right between her breasts. Now she was positively overheated.

"You know, I wouldn't mind a little help with Erika."

"Huh?" She'd been so busy thinking about him licking her that she missed the essence of what he was saying.

"Maybe she'll open up to you. Female to female. I'm out of my depth on this one. I would appreciate your advice."

Wow! "I'd be glad to do anything I can."

He looked at the ground, almost as if he were uncomfortable. "She's growing up fast. I think there are...some things I'm not fully prepared to deal with."

"Like what?"

He chuckled, then shook his head. "Female things." Dragging his hand down his face, he covered his mouth with splayed fingers and simply looked at her.

"Oh."

"We've done *the* talk, and I thought I'd crumble to dust. I'm not sure I can handle it when...she becomes a woman."

Men. They were so darn cute. Her mom had given her *the* talk, and her father had absolutely, unequivocally refused to ever purchase feminine products for any reason for any woman. Ever. "I can help Erika with that when the time comes."

"Thank you."

She gathered her Baggie and the empty soda can, then rolled to her hands and knees facing him. And stopped. The enormity of what he'd given her overwhelmed her. "Thank you. You can't imagine how honored I am to be given this important duty."

"I think you're making fun of me." Then his eyes dropped, and she realized that in this position her tank top wasn't flush with her body. And she was giving him an eyeful.

She stood, grabbed the pack, shoved her litter inside then handed it to Tanner. A flush shot up from her breasts to her throat to her face.

Turning, she surveyed the tree line with her back to him. Amid the rustle of plastic and the clink of the cans, she put her hands on her hips and tipped her head. Fluffy had been in an oak, the body beneath, the meadow to the left, though the tree had seemed to be right on the edge of it. They'd trudged around the rim, right next to the trees, but maybe they needed to go deeper in the forest, change the angle. Cats *did* see differently than humans, and she might have misjudged.

The rustling stopped. She glanced over her shoulder to find Tanner standing a few steps away, the pack dangling from his fingers. He wasn't surveying the land. He was staring at her.

Then he dropped the pack, closed the distance between them, grabbed her arm and hauled her up against him.

"I shouldn't do this. But it's all I've been thinking about for the last hour. So I have to."

He didn't just kiss her, he devoured her. Holding her still with one hand cupping her head, his other arm wrapped across her back, he plundered her mouth like a Viking warrior. She slid her fingers into the hair at his nape. His chest was hard, his hair soft and his tongue hot and sizzling in her mouth. He smelled like sun-dried laundry, the subtle zest of cologne and heady male hormones. Dipping his knees, he plunged deeper, backed off to nip her lip, then angled in the opposite direction to take her all over again.

He made a sound, a low, intimate growl deep in his throat, then his hand slipped down to the curve of her butt and pressed her against him. Oh, Lord, he was hard. She wanted—

"I won't have any salacious activities going on in my backyard, you heathens."

Lili jumped and stumbled two steps before Tanner caught her. Then she saw the shotgun pointed straight at them.

HIS COCK WAS HARDER THAN a diamond-tipped drill bit. All he could think about was her. Holy hell, he was in trouble.

Tanner shoved Lili behind him. "Buddy, put that gun down. You know you aren't going to shoot us."

Buddy Welch had them in his sights, and his finger trembled on the trigger of his twelve-gauge. "You're trespassing."

"You know this is public land."

"I don't recognize a government that takes my land away."

Buddy Welch was the picture of a mountain man if there ever was one. His pink scalp peeked through sparse white hair that hadn't seen a comb since the Vietnam War. Streaks of dirt filled the craggy lines along his nose, and a grizzled gray beard reached his chest. Faded camouflage pants and an old flak jacket completed the look. The old man was a relic from the war, *one* of the wars, though Tanner wasn't sure which, only that Buddy Welch had been living in a shack in the middle of his three acres long before Tanner had moved in. He was a fixture, though the government hadn't taken the land from him, as Buddy claimed. The meadow and forest had always been public land.

Nor had Buddy shot anyone, not even a real trespasser. The old man liked to threaten. It usually worked, too.

Lili gripped Tanner's shoulders and tried to peer around him. "Stay back there," Tanner whispered, his gaze never leaving Buddy. Then he raised his voice once more. "You know you don't want the county sheriff out here. Gresswell might seize your illegal firepower again."

"I don't have anything illegal. They're registered

with the laaaw." He gave the word extra emphasis, then spat in the grass.

"All right. Then I'll appeal to your sense of chivalry. You're frightening my friend."

"She didn't *look* scared when I first saw her."

Lili clung to his back, but whether it was from fright or embarrassment at what they'd been caught doing, he wasn't sure. If Buddy had shown up five minutes later, they'd have been horizontal on the ground with only the soft grass as a cushion.

Tanner hadn't been thinking too clearly from the moment she'd rolled to her hands and knees in front of him.

"Well, she's scared now. So put the damn gun down."

Then Buddy suddenly raised the rifle in the air and pulled the trigger. Instead of a blast, there was a click. The gun hadn't been loaded.

"Goddamn buzzards." Buddy spat in the grass again.

Behind him, Lili made a little horrified *eww* noise. "He's not chewing tobacco, is he?" she whispered.

"*That*—" he pointed at Buddy "—wasn't nice."

Buddy took it to mean firing the shotgun to scare the crap out of them. "Next time it'll be loaded, and I'll be firing at buzzards of the human variety." Then he slapped the gun on his shoulder, turned and marched across the meadow.

Keeping her hands on him, Lili shuffled to Tanner's side. "I thought he was just an urban legend around here."

Tanner pulled Lili under his arm. "Are you okay?"

She smiled lopsidedly up at him. "I'm fine." She covered her mouth. "Oops. I mean I'm totally peachy."

Tanner turned. Her fingers slid across his back, then

fell away. He wanted her to keep touching him. "I got out of hand—"

She put a finger to his lips. He had the overpowering urge to suck it into his mouth.

"I liked your kiss. A lot. So don't apologize, okay?"

Her lips were plump and well kissed. He was pretty sure her dilated pupils hadn't been caused by fright, and he was damn sure her tight, beaded nipples had nothing to do with fear. His fingers had mussed her hair, tangling the fine strands. Needing his hands on her, he smoothed them back to order.

"You," he said, then let out a heavy sigh, because somehow she made him breathless all over again, "have a way of making me forget where I am and what I'm supposed to be doing."

Turning her face, she nuzzled into his hand. "Ditto." Then she pulled away. "Tanner, did he say *buzzards?*" Then she tipped her face to the sky. "Oh, my God, there *are* buzzards."

He turned, first his head on his shoulders, so slowly he could hear the creak of his neck, then his whole body. And watched a flock of buzzards circling over the trees. He felt a little queasy. "It could be an animal."

She didn't even bother to answer that. "How long have they been there?" she whispered.

"I don't know." Buzzards were the first thing he should have looked for. If he'd truly believed.

There were only three, but they were buzzards. Not crows or blue jays or sparrows. Then one dive-bombed, straight down.

Tanner's stomach dive-bombed right along with it.

"You go look," she said, giving him a slight push.

It never occurred to him to take her along. "Will you be all right out here alone?"

She nodded. "Better than I will be if I go in there."

He glanced back over his shoulder as Buddy Welch disappeared into the thicket on the other side of the field. "I won't be long. But you yell like hell if he comes back."

"Okay."

He studied the vultures once more. From the ground, it was difficult to gauge how far in their quarry lay. Then he entered the forest. Dark and cool beneath the trees, the ground was moist. He couldn't find a path in the underbrush, so he made his own, glancing up when the sky peeked through the canopy to make sure he was on a beeline for the buzzards.

Lions and tigers and bears! Oh my! He had to smile, thinking of Dorothy in the forest with the Tin Man and the Scarecrow. The movie had been Erika's favorite until she watched *Napoleon Dynamite.* Quite frankly, he didn't get the switch in allegiance. In fact, he hadn't even understood the movie. But Erika knew every line and said it before each character did.

And thinking about Erika was better than thinking about… The deeper he went, the more elemental the scents became. Decaying leaves, wet soil, animal droppings. And something else.

He shoved aside a branch only to have the one in front of it whack him in the face.

That smell. What the hell was it? He could actually taste it. Like shrimp that had gone bad. Or…

He was afraid to take a deep breath. He was actually afraid to push through the bushes. But he did.

Aw, shit.

There were more than three buzzards.

And animals didn't wear bright blue windbreakers.

CHAPTER NINE

HE WAS A MAN. HE WASN'T going to be sick. But he'd never before seen anything this bad. Animals had dragged…it. He didn't want to think of it as a once living, breathing person. Now it was…parts. It wasn't even completely intact.

Tanner picked up a rock, threw it, and the vultures dispersed into the sky. Bile rose in his throat, and if he didn't get the hell out now, he was going to be sick.

Lili stood in the meadow right where he'd left her. A statue. Only her hair blowing gently in the afternoon breeze. Tanner stayed in the shadow of a tree where she couldn't easily see him and used his cell phone. She didn't move the entire time it took to make the call and pinpoint their location as best he could. Just her hair, wafting back and forth across her shoulders, into her face, and away again.

Then he stepped into the bright sunlight. Lili simply collapsed onto her haunches.

He hunkered down beside her. Thin blue lines showed beneath the pale skin of her cheeks. A pulse ticked at her throat.

She rocked slowly. "It was really there, wasn't it?"

Even she called what he'd found an *it*. "Don't think about it. I want you to go home." No, wait, he didn't want her walking by herself. He'd lose a lifetime thinking about her alone in the woods. Anything could happen. "Stay with me. The police will be here soon, *then* I'll take you home."

"Tanner?"

That was all she said. Looking at him as if he had answers for…something, the horror of murder so close to home.

What the hell had he done? He hadn't given a single thought to what this outcome would do to Lili. He'd treated the whole episode as some itch to get out of her system. Placate her, show her she's wrong, move on. He'd damn near made love to her with that thing mere yards away in the woods.

Good Lord. Erika. How the hell was he supposed to tell his daughter? If Lili was traumatized, Erika would be comatose.

He was the screw-up of the century.

Yet Lili was looking at him as if he had the answers.

"I don't feel so well," she murmured.

He cupped her cheek, her skin clammy and cold. "Come here." He folded her into his arms.

"I didn't think it was real. I mean, I know what Fluffy saw, but I sort of stopped thinking about it being a real person." She didn't cry, but she hiccuped. "It was just a body that had to be found," she whispered. Then she raised her head from his shoulder to meet his eyes. "Does that make sense?"

"Yeah." TV desensitized a person to violence. It was a concept rather than a reality. Until it got slammed into your face. Tanner couldn't get that smell out of his nostrils or the phantom taste out of his mouth.

He'd only felt this kind of helplessness once, the day Karen had died, the moment when he'd gone from an angry "What the hell has she done?" to a panicked "Dear God, this can't be happening."

Yet, with the sun on his head, the cheerful chirp of a nearby bird, Lili's face once again pressed to his shoulder and her flowery scent driving that freaking smell away, he'd never felt closer to a human soul.

It was as terrifying as the first time he'd held Erika in his arms.

LILI FOLLOWED IN TANNER'S wake across the meadow. Since they'd started out earlier in the day, the sun had tracked across the sky, and everything, *everything* was different. She wasn't the same person she'd been two hours, a can of soda and a tuna-fish sandwich ago.

Lili couldn't believe it. There really was a body. It wasn't an *it*. That was a man lying out there.

She closed her eyes and shuddered.

The police had been out there looking for clues for fifteen minutes, or half an hour…or more. She'd lost track of time while more cops had arrived, then Sheriff Gresswell. They hadn't called it murder, but Lili knew that it was. It was now more than something Fluffy had seen. She'd answered what felt like a zillion questions, but when she'd opened her mouth to tell them about Fluffy, Tanner had given her a look. *Don't.* That was his unspoken message, and she got it loud and clear. Why she'd obeyed, she couldn't say. That was why she felt guilty now. Not mentioning Fluffy felt like a lie of omission.

Tanner had finally gotten them dispensation to go home.

They moved from meadow and sunshine onto the woods path that would lead them to her backyard. She shuddered again in the sudden coolness of the shade.

She didn't realize she'd made an accompanying sound until Tanner turned, took hold of her shoulders and leaned down to read her face. "Are you all right?"

She remembered the way he'd held her in the meadow before the police had arrived, as if they were the only two people in the world and they needed each other. This was an altogether different Tanner. Despite the seeming concern in his question, his fingers bit a little too deeply.

She opened her mouth to ask him what was wrong, what had changed, why he was looking at her as if she'd *done* something, but another thought flew into her head. "Where's Einstein?" She clapped a hand over her mouth. "Oh, God, I forgot all about her."

"The cat's fine. It's at—"

The fact that he'd cut himself off made her stomach tumble. "Where is she?"

"You don't want to know."

Translation: she was making a nuisance of herself at the…crime scene.

"Einstein will be back." Tanner smoothed his hands along her arms, but he stared over her shoulder as if his mind was…back there.

"Why didn't we tell them about Fluffy?" she whispered.

His gaze shot to her face. "It'll confuse the issue."

"But they don't even know it's a murder yet. I have

to tell them or they won't figure it out until they do the autopsy."

He dipped his head, and the soothing caress of his hands ceased. "There are—" He squeezed her arms. "They can tell a lot of things before the autopsy merely by looking. And since I don't think they're stupid, I do think they'll *look*."

"Oh." She sucked in a breath between her clenched teeth. Tanner had left her in the meadow for a time while he'd shown the two sheriff's deputies the exact location. "Oh," she said again, and that was the most she could manage.

"We want to keep a low profile, Lili." He spoke as if to a child.

She felt like a child, totally inept, clueless and bewildered. "They won't know exactly where it happened." Fluffy had been in a tree much closer to the meadow than where Tanner had found…the remains.

"They'll figure it out."

"But how?"

"Don't ask me how, okay?" His voice was sharper, his grip harder. He was trying to shield her from the details, but there was only one answer. Drag marks. She didn't want to throw up; she just wanted to go to sleep.

But she couldn't run away from it. "Fluffy's a witness."

"Fluffy's a cat, not a witness." Tanner shook her. "Do you honestly think they're going to believe you?"

Tanner hadn't believed her, so why would the police? That was why she hadn't gone to them in the first place. Yet hearing Tanner say it was like poking a finger in an open wound.

He *kept* poking. "They're not going to give a damn

what you *say* Fluffy saw. So we're going to leave it alone." Then he must have realized how hard, how angry he sounded, because he once again smoothed up and down her arms. "This is the best way. The police are good at what they do."

"I don't feel right about this, Tanner."

He straightened and stepped away from her altogether, turning for a moment so she couldn't see his eyes, couldn't read his expression, couldn't fathom what he was thinking. Then he delivered the death blow over his shoulder. "Do you want to get Erika involved in all this?"

Of course. That had been his concern from the get-go, and she'd ignored it. Good Lord, it was a mess. She hadn't thought about the ramifications. She'd actually been happy that he'd told Roscoe and Erika what Fluffy had shown her. *Happy.* She was an idiot human, just as Einstein liked to point out.

How would Erika ever recover from this horrible thing? Lili couldn't do anything about the body; that was out there, and so was a murderer. But by insisting Tanner *had* to help her, she'd brought the horror of it right into the Rutland house.

"We took a hike, we saw Buddy, then the buzzards, then I went into the woods to look," Tanner repeated the story they'd given the police as if she required a reminder. "That's the important information. The rest is just..."

Just what, Tanner? She didn't ask. She didn't want to know what he thought of her. "What about Buddy? Maybe we shouldn't have told them about him, either. What if they accuse him of killing that man just because he happened to be there?"

"Give them some credit. They'd need more evidence

than that. And maybe Buddy saw something. Either today or earlier if he was out there."

Lili suddenly remembered Lady Dreadlock lying in the long grass. Would the police jump to conclusions about her? Definitely. The woman talked to animals, but Einstein didn't get a freaky impression from her, which the cat certainly would have received if Lady D. had killed someone. There was something else going on with the woman that had nothing to do with murder, Lili was sure of it. She couldn't throw her to the dogs before she'd had time to think through all the implications. That was the problem with everything she'd done so far; she hadn't considered every outcome *before* she took action.

She almost laughed aloud, maybe a little hysterically. She'd castigated Tanner for not telling the police about Fluffy, and here she was taking it upon herself to shield Lady Dreadlock simply because the woman could talk to animals.

"Lili?" Tanner tipped her chin. "Where'd you go?"

"I was thinking."

"About what?" A furrow marred his brow, and his usually open blue gaze was hooded and unreadable.

"I was thinking that I need to be strong for Erika." It wasn't exactly a lie, but not the whole truth, either. Still, she had to stare at his shoulder as she uttered it. "Right now, I can't think much further ahead than that."

The shadows clouding his eyes deepened. "Believe it or not, I can't, either."

HE COULD HEAR LILI'S SOFT footfalls behind him and actually felt it inside every time she sighed. Ahead he could see her back fence at the end of the path. They were almost home. He had to decide how to handle Erika. Tanner regretted telling her what Lili claimed Fluffy saw. That decision had been made under the erroneous assumption that there was no body.

The body changed everything.

While he wanted his daughter to exercise her brain and think for herself, there was no way in hell he'd let her anywhere near a murder investigation. Not even peripherally.

Lili simply didn't get it. The police were not going to ask her to help them solve the crime by *talking* to Fluffy and getting more information. They'd start investigating *her.* Then they'd get around to questioning Erika about everything that had happened from the moment she'd taken Fluffy next door.

He would not have his daughter questioned.

In the back of his mind, he could hear the way his thoughts had altered. He was back to referring to what Lili *claimed* Fluffy knew; what Lili *said* happened. That brief moment of oneness he'd felt had been snuffed out by the stench in the air as he'd led the deputies into the woods. It was in his hair, on his clothes, up his nostrils. The rancid aroma of death.

And he'd had the unconscionable thought that maybe Lili had known the body was there *before* she'd talked to Fluffy.

He'd started watching her, observing the long minutes of brooding silence. Yes, finding the body bothered her, but as the afternoon wore on, her silences wore on him until everything she said and did became suspicious. He'd become certain she was hiding something that moment on the path when she couldn't meet his eyes. She hadn't been thinking about Erika, he was sure of that, so what the hell *was* she thinking about?

THE RUTLAND KITCHEN WAS LIGHT blue with lace curtains at the window over the sink. It was neat and fairly up to date with an automatic ice maker and water dispenser in the refrigerator door. The blue-and-white checkerboard tablecloth matched the wall paint, and a small jelly jar of yellow daises sat in the middle of the table. It wasn't the sort of thing you'd expect to find in a male-dominated household, but then Roscoe wasn't your typical grandfather, and Lili was sure he was the family decorator.

It gave Lili the heebie-jeebies to be resting her elbows on the checkerboard cloth while the four of them talked about dead bodies, as if the discussion would forever taint the friendly kitchen. Yet it was the way Tanner kept looking at her that made her stomach roil and rumble. He had penetrating ice-blue eyes, the eyes of a predator waiting for its prey's weakest moment.

Erika didn't seem to notice the tension at all. "So Lili really can talk to animals?" It was just like a child to skip over the horrific bits and glom on to the unimportant and innocuous parts. "Wow. That's pretty cool."

Tanner's eyebrows dipped together, and he drummed his fingers on the table. Erika's gaze ping-ponged from her father to Lili. If Lili didn't miss her guess, there was steam starting to come out of Tanner's ears, and his voice held the strain of keeping a tight rein on himself. "There's nothing cool about it, Erika." He glanced at Lili. "*Murder* isn't cool."

That glance set a little warning bell going inside her.

The fact that Tanner had to qualify the statement meant he *had* been thinking animal speak wasn't cool. Yet right now, the thing of utmost importance was to lend her support. For Erika's sake. "Something terrible has happened to a human being. It's not a TV show you're watching. This is real now."

"I know," Erika said, her eyes as bright blue as the tablecloth. "There's a bad person out there. I mean, there's lots of bad people, but this one came really close to our house. And he could still be out there."

Okay, so Erika *was* getting it.

"But I'm glad about one thing."

How could anyone be glad about anything? Maybe Lili should have let Tanner handle the conversation without offering her two cents. He looked at her, waiting for her brilliant comeback.

Erika gave an expectant little rise to her blond eyebrows.

"What are you glad about?" Lili finally managed to say. Yeah, a truly brilliant comeback.

"Well, you know how you see those real-life detective shows, where the family can't get over their kidnapped child because they don't know what happened to them?"

It brought a hollow ache to her chest. Lili didn't like to watch those kinds of TV shows, and she was surprised Tanner let Erika watch them. "Yes."

"Well, if it were me, I'd rather know and not keep hoping forever for something that isn't going to happen."

Across from her, Tanner made a movement, or perhaps a sound. His Adam's apple bobbed as he swallowed once, then again. Roscoe shoved a glass of water into his hand.

"That's very wise." Lili patted Erika's arm. If there was any brilliance around here, it was coming from this remarkable child. "I think I'd want to know, too."

"So," Erika said, glancing at each adult in turn, including Roscoe, "what are we going to do to help find the murderer?"

Lili exchanged a look with Tanner. He gave her a stern do-not-open-your-mouth look and dealt with the subject himself. "*We* aren't doing anything. We'll let the police do their job."

"But, Dad, what about what Fluffy saw?"

Lili was glad Fluffy had been relegated to Erika's bedroom for the duration of the discussion. Right about now, Erika would have tossed the cat at her and expected her to solve everything.

Tanner had his own moment of truth to handle. "The police don't know anything about Fluffy," he said.

"But, Dad." Erika's voice held a tone of awe and disbelief. "Isn't it lying not to tell them?"

A hush fell over the kitchen. Erika waited. Roscoe waited. Lili ached that she was the cause of that note in Erika's voice. In the distance, she could hear a siren. She didn't think it had anything to do with the scene in the woods, because, well, that didn't need a siren. Yet it was a haunting sound that raised goose bumps along her arms.

Tanner didn't try to wiggle out of the cold, hard fact. "Yes. And I'm taking full responsibility for lying." He leaned down and looked pointedly at Erika. "I'm not getting you involved in this. That's my decision. Do I make myself clear?"

Erika folded her hands in her lap. "Yes, Dad."

"I don't want you to play in the woods alone."

"You never let me play in the woods alone anyway."

"I want you to stick close to home, and keep your cell phone charged. You remember how to call emergency, right?

Erika rolled her eyes. "I am twelve years old, you know."

He hooked his thumb along his jawline, curled his fingers against his lips and looked at her for several deep breaths. Erika put her hand over her own mouth in imitation and gave him back the same studied look. His eyes were the same shade as hers, the same shape, and they had the same type-A circles.

"I love you, and I don't want anything bad to happen to you." He reached out and linked pinkies with his precious daughter. "I would die if something happened to you."

"Ditto, Dad. I'm sorry if I sounded like I was minimizing the seriousness of the situation."

Lili would have laughed—it sounded so like a repeat of something Tanner would say—but she felt like an outsider in this most intimate of moments between father and daughter.

"I know you don't like to have to tell a lie," Erika said with equal seriousness, belied a moment later by a growing twinkle in her eye. "I promise that I won't throw it back in your face when *I* tell a lie."

Tanner wagged their linked fingers. "You will *not* tell lies."

Lili ached to take both their hands and become part of their circle. Kate had asked her if she wanted children—could that have been only this morning? It had been a future thing, like the idea of finding a body.

A concept, something without an emotional attachment to it. Watching Tanner and his daughter, the concept morphed into a need.

Her carelessness had jeopardized what these two shared. Maybe the crisis had been averted for the moment, but she'd dealt thoughtlessly with the *concept* of murder. As easily as Erika seemed to accept what had happened, that didn't mean the event wouldn't have lasting effects on her, traumatizing effects. But Tanner had put Erika first, and Lili suddenly had an inkling of what it meant to be a parent. The joy and the agony. The fear that you'd make a mistake. The horror if you failed to protect.

He'd asked her to help him talk to Erika. Lili was suddenly afraid she didn't have a clue what to say to the child about anything. She'd make a terrible muddle. She'd be awful—

SPAM, SPAM SPAM! The image was in her head first, then she saw Einstein, stomach splayed against the screen door, clinging by all four paws almost as if the cat were suspended in midair.

"What the hell?" Roscoe exclaimed.

Lili jumped up. Whether Einstein was talking about food or making a reference to the nature of Lili's muddled thoughts wasn't clear, but the cat would ruin the screen with her claws.

Get down. Lili accompanied that with an image of a broomstick, though she'd never swat an animal with a broomstick.

"Grandpa, you shouldn't swear."

"That wasn't swearing. It was an involuntary exclamation."

Tanner rounded on Erika. "And that doesn't mean you're allowed to have involuntary exclamations because your grandfather sometimes does."

Einstein sprang backward, catapulting off the screen and landing feet-first on the porch. There were numerous little holes in the screen. Einstein would need fifteen sets of claws to make that many holes.

"I'm so sorry about what she did to your door."

"Don't worry," Roscoe said. "Fluffy likes to hang out on the screen, too."

There was something about cats and screen doors and food. No matter how intelligent they were, they lost all sense of decorum.

Einstein was her cue to leave. She'd done enough to the Rutland family. She opened the door and backed out. "It's time for me to feed everyone back at my house."

"Dinner will be ready in an hour," Roscoe said. "Why don't you come?"

Lili looked from Erika's hopeful gaze to Tanner. He had that look again, a hard, assessing quality, the line between his brows more distinct than usual, his eyes closer to a stormy gray than a cordial blue. Tanner didn't second the invitation.

Lili felt twitchy all over again.

"Thanks, Roscoe, but once I settle the cats, they don't like me to leave." The excuse sounded hokey even to her, but she couldn't sit across from Tanner's stare through an entire meal.

"If you change your mind, pop over. I'm making lasagna. And I do make the best lasagna." Roscoe chucked Erika under the chin. "Right, honey?"

"Right, Grandpa."

Tanner stared. Lili let the screen door shut. "Thanks."

She backed off the porch. It was the oddest feeling, seeing them through the screen, like watching a TV. She wasn't a part of it. Her life was here on the outside, theirs on the inside.

She turned and almost tripped over Einstein. Grabbing up the cat, she scooted to the hole in the hedge, popping through to the other side just as a tidal wave of cat images filled her mind.

They came so furiously she wasn't even able to put words to them. But she knew exactly what Einstein was telling her.

Holding the cat aloft, she stared.

"So they know," she whispered.

As Tanner said, the police weren't dumb. They'd figured it was murder, and they'd found the spot where it had happened.

"Einstein, you're the best. Now you need to tell me what to do about Tanner and Erika."

What Einstein said about Tanner wasn't repeatable.

ROSCOE CIRCLED HIS THUMB around a water tumbler. "Is Lili okay?"

"Lili? What about Erika?"

"Erika's fine, Tanner."

Tanner had sent her upstairs to get ready for supper. "Are you letting her watch Court TV after school?"

"Of course not," Roscoe said, concentrating on his tumbler.

"Then what was that about kidnapped children?"

"Afternoon cartoons."

That was a load of crap. Though cartoons could be

violent. Look at the Road Runner always setting off bombs right next to Wile E. Coyote. He did have to admit there was a certain sense of wisdom to what Erika had said. She was a sensible girl, the way he wanted her to be. She'd keep her phone with her, she wouldn't talk to strangers and she wouldn't wander off alone.

But Tanner had taught his daughter that lying was okay. Part of him wanted to resent Lili for that, but the decision had been his alone.

Roscoe took a sip of water, then said, "Does Lili realize you didn't tell the police as much to protect her as Erika?"

"It had nothing to do with Lili."

His father cocked a white eyebrow.

The police wouldn't have believed a cat had told Lili about a murder *it* had witnessed. The investigation would have become all about her. That was when he'd made the decision to keep silent, despite his own doubts about what she knew, what she was hiding and... "How *did* Lili know that body was there?"

Roscoe rose from the table, opened the oven door, then closed it again. "I take it you don't think Fluffy told her."

"Do you?"

"I don't know, Tanner." He crumpled a bit of tinfoil in his fist. "But I know she didn't have anything to do with putting that body there."

"I never said that." But had the thought actually crossed his mind? In all the jumble of thoughts and emotions he'd been feeling, he couldn't remember thinking *that*. He stood up simply because he had to move.

Roscoe tossed the used foil into the trash under the sink. "If Fluffy didn't tell her, then that's the only other explanation, isn't it? Yet if she did have something to do with it—" Tanner noticed Roscoe avoided putting the words *Lili* and *murder* together "—then why would she tell us about it? It'd be more likely that she'd want to keep it a secret."

"Not if what she was trying to prove all along was that she can talk to animals." He'd wondered more than once what Lili got out of telling the story. "What if she found it while she was walking and decided it was the perfect way to get everyone to believe in her?"

"I don't think Lili's that devious. Why can't you just believe?"

Because he required proof, as his daughter did, but Erika wasn't as suspicious as Tanner was. Her trustfulness hadn't plummeted to the point where she'd consider Lili devious enough to come up with a plan like that, but trust was a double-edged sword. You didn't want your child to lose faith in human nature, but you also didn't want her to accept every Tom, Dick and Harry that came her way. Wasn't teaching her that lesson the reason behind telling her Lili's tale in the first place?

That had sure backfired on him.

"You want to hear why I think you don't want to believe?"

"You'll tell me even if I say no." Tanner opened the fridge and pulled out one of Roscoe's leftover beers from the previous night. "So I'm all ears."

"You're afraid of her." Roscoe held up a hand when Tanner started to sputter out an answer. "You can't categorize her. She's illogical and impractical, and you can't predict what she's going to do next."

She was all of those things and more, many of which

he admired. "What does that have to do with whether she talks to animals or not?"

"Nothing. But if she's illogical and unpredictable, you can't control her. And if you can't control her, that means you can't keep her safe. So it's easier for you to believe she has some ulterior motive for the whole thing."

Tanner clenched his back teeth. He would not get pissed at his dad. He would remain rational. Logical and practical. "That is the biggest load of bullshit you've ever spouted, Roscoe, and believe me, I've heard you spout one helluva lot of bullshit in your day."

"I'm telling you what I think."

The beer bottle seemed to heat in his grasp. He set it on the table without slamming it down. "I'm sure she's perfectly capable of keeping herself safe."

"If she can take care of herself, then why not tell the police that she said Fluffy told her about the body?" Roscoe cocked his hip against the counter. "Go ahead, tell me that it had nothing to do with protecting her."

Tanner simply took a slug of beer.

"You didn't tell them because you didn't want them to get into anything that would make them think Lili had something to do with what happened to that fellow out in the woods."

"They wouldn't have thought that."

"That's exactly what they would have thought, and *you*—" Roscoe pointed his finger "—didn't want them to even go there."

"Fine. So I don't want them to go there. My concern is how that would affect Erika."

"Now who's bullshitting who?"

"Roscoe, check your lasagna. And kindly mind your own business."

"Said like a man who's afraid to face the truth." But Roscoe did open the oven for a look.

It was all a bunch of psychological claptrap. It didn't even hit home with his reasons for not wanting Karen to go on that Sedona trip. That had been all about Erika. So why did icy fingers stroke down his spine? "Maybe the simple truth is that I don't want to look like an idiot by telling the police that my cat said there was a body."

Roscoe merely smiled. "You've never minded looking like an idiot before." Before Tanner could find a good comeback for that one, Roscoe added, "Do you want garlic bread with this?"

"A salad is fine."

The conversation was thankfully over for now, but Roscoe's continued smile said Tanner hadn't heard the last of it.

The sooner he tackled Lili regarding what she was hiding, the better. He needed, however, to be calm and rational by the time he did it.

CHAPTER TEN

LILI TOOK A SIP OF WINE. She'd forced Tanner to lie, then brought him down a few pegs in his daughter's eyes because he had to admit his transgression. She'd been afraid to even talk to Fluffy in case she couldn't understand, or in case she could and what he told her was worse than before. All in all, she wasn't batting a thousand today, and if she really thought about it, there were probably quite a few more things she'd screwed up.

Einstein jumped up on Wanetta's scratchy old burgundy sofa and laid her head in Lili's lap. Einstein was the furthest thing from a lap cat, yet she set a sweet purr rumbling against Lili's tummy, kneaded without putting her claws out and thankfully kept her thoughts to herself.

Of course, Einstein could get pretty user-friendly when she wanted something, and she did love cheese. Lili rewarded her with a piece even if it was bad for her teeth.

Don Juan jumped on the back of the sofa and sniffed. An elegant Siamese, he adored the ladies, but he loved cheese, too. All the cats did.

"All right, you can have a piece, but you have to get off Wanetta's doily."

Don Juan was no dummy, scooting over to remove

his back paws from the handmade lace. Lili gave him the cheese.

Wanetta had left Lili the furnishings as well as the house, and that included all her knickknacks, handmade doilies, African violets, the heavy drapes that Lili had pulled to shut out the darkness and the imitation Tiffany lamps that glowed softly.

Bash bumped Lili's calf. Short for Bashful, the calico female was anything but. Another irony. Bash loved cuddling and petting. She should have been the easiest one to find a home for, but Lili had been striking out all over the place. She gave Bash a piece, too, until finally all the cats were whining for their cheese. Lili only had two pieces left for herself.

She'd risen from the couch and was halfway to the kitchen when she heard the knock on the back door and saw a man's outline against the screen. Not just any man. Tanner.

The cats, all but Einstein, vanished like Houdini's helpers.

She felt a little earthquake in her chest. She was sure he had a lot to say to her. More than she wanted to hear.

"I'm a woman, I can take it," she whispered, then raised her voice. "Come in. We're in the living room."

Maybe she shouldn't have said *we,* since to him Einstein was an *it.* She hid her wineglass behind an African violet on one of Wanetta's myriad tables strewn about the room.

She wasn't prepared for him in Wanetta's frilly living room. He smelled so good, and he was so tall he seemed to fill the space with more than his body. He filled it with his presence, all male, all comfort. For a moment Lili wished they were back in the meadow when he'd been kissing her, before Buddy had threatened them with his gun, before they'd seen the vultures, before Tanner had gone alone into the woods. She wished they were still kissing and the rest had never happened.

She stepped forward and put her hand over his mouth before he could get out a word.

THE CAT STARED AT HIM, flicked its tail, then jumped from the back of the couch and sauntered off to the hinterlands of the house's interior.

Thank God. Because Lili's touch short-circuited Tanner's brain.

"Before you say anything, I have to get this off my chest."

God, she was going to tell him her secret before he could even ask. Her trust made his heart turn over. Though he did wish she'd found it earlier.

"I'm so sorry I made you tell that lie. I know you did it to protect Erika, but it's all my fault."

"You didn't—"

She pressed harder. Her flowery perfume, the feel of her fingers against his lips and the soulfulness in her eyes made him forget every doubt he'd had. She'd lit some candles to blanket the room with a sweet, spicy scent, closed the drapes, and where the room had been relaxing while Wanetta had presided, Lili charged the atmosphere with seduction. He was equally sure she didn't have a clue about that.

"Shh," she said, "it's my turn. No contradictions until I'm done. Nod once for yes."

He nodded. What else could a man do but give in?

She took a deep breath, and she was so close, he felt the brush of her exhalation against his skin.

"Okay. I didn't think about how all this would affect Erika. I wanted you to help me." She tapped her chest. "*Me*. It wasn't about Fluffy or Erika. It was about what I needed. And because of that, you ended up having to make Erika party to the lie we told. I'm not sure whether we should tell the police or not, but I never meant for you to go against your parenting principles. And I'm so sorry."

He waited a beat but she didn't go on. "Are you done?"

"I'm not sure. No, wait, there's more." She stepped back and twisted her hands. "I think this might actually be worse."

"Lili—"

"Let me get it out." She rubbed her stomach as if it hurt.

He'd wanted to read her the riot act. He'd wanted to make demands. Yet she disarmed the anger with her innocence. That was the only word he could think of. She was innocent like Erika, with a simple lack of guile that was distinctively Lili.

Roscoe was right. Lili couldn't be devious enough to lie about Fluffy or the body. Or anything at all.

"Spit it out, Lili."

"I was happy when you told Erika about my talk with Fluffy. There, I said it. I was happy. I didn't even think about how Erika might feel. I can't believe I did that." She turned away, bobbing her head as if she couldn't find words vile enough to describe what she'd done. "I knew I had to do something after what Fluffy told me, but I did all the wrong things."

He stroked a hand up her back. Not touching her wasn't an option. Her blouse rode up, revealing a strip of skin along the waistband of her skirt. She'd changed after what had happened that afternoon, but she'd found an equally tantalizing outfit.

"Now are you done?" he asked, a huskiness to his voice he didn't even recognize.

His hand traveled beneath the fall of hair, and he caressed the nape of her neck, the smooth, delicate skin. Dropping a kiss on the fragrant flesh between her throat and shoulder seemed the most natural thing in the world.

He took her silence as a yes. "Then it's my turn."

He pressed his body along her back and held her against him with a hand on her shoulder. "*I* told Erika about Fluffy. *I* decided not to tell the police. If Erika learned a poor lesson today, *I* taught it to her. You didn't have any part in that."

He wrapped an arm across her abdomen. He wanted the warm length of her body against his, all of it, all of her.

"Sometimes there are justifiable reasons to lie," he went on. "She's smart enough to realize this was one of them."

She turned her head, her hair sliding across his hand, and hit him with the full impact of her lilac eyes. "I'm not sure—"

"I'm sure. None of this is your fault. I told the lie because I needed to. I wouldn't do it any differently." He cupped her face, smoothed his finger over her cheek.

Nothing else mattered but making her believe that. Her lips were like wine he thirsted for.

She moaned against his mouth and turned in his arms, the slip-slide of her body firing every nerve ending. He tipped her head back and drank her in, tasting the headiness of a desire he hadn't felt in a long, long time. Dipping, he gathered her closer, lifted her higher, until she wrapped her arms around his neck and opened completely.

The taste of her was like no other, uniquely Lili, as lush as the bouquet of flowers she'd given him. The sounds she made strummed his skin and set a fire burning in his belly.

He let her feet touch the floor, dipped once again and rode up beneath her blouse, his fingers tracing the indentations of her spine, gliding over all that smooth skin. He cupped her sides and pressed his thumbs up between their bodies to find the underside of her breasts, then the hard, cherried nipples.

Trapping his face in her palms, holding his mouth captive, she pulled back to give him what he wanted— free rein of her breasts. He pushed her bra up and took handfuls of sweet, soft Lili. A mouthful of lush Lili. Her lips, her tongue. She drove him to the brink.

He rubbed against her, but it wasn't enough. Sliding one hand down to her butt, he held her close and rocked his erection between their bodies. He bunched her skirt in his fist and raised it until he could hold the firm globe of her bottom in his hand, and it wasn't enough. He wouldn't get enough until he was buried deep inside her.

He withdrew far enough to whisper, "I need to touch you."

Her eyes were wide, dark pools, and Lili spoke without words, guiding his hand to the elastic of her panties. He found his own way beneath the lace as she raised a leg and wrapped it around his knee. More than enough room to glide inside her warmth. She was slick and creamy, her clitoris already a hard, needy button. He bent her slightly over his arm, bracing her even as she dug her nails into his biceps and let her head fall back. She moaned softly as he circled her, then slid inside. Nipping her neck, licking the hollow of her throat, he made love to her with his fingers, first one, then two, until her body moved with his, rocked with him as if he were buried deep inside her. And with each upward stroke, he hit her clitoris, gliding over it, then back inside.

He knew she was close when she threw her arms around his neck and clung to him, her breath hot against his ear. He went for the button, circling it, until she shuddered in his arms, and her voice threaded through her breath, turning into soft moans.

Her sounds, her skin, her heat, the very essence of her put him on the verge of climax himself.

Then she bit his throat lightly and came.

Her orgasm was so elemental, so pure, so profound, he damn near came with her.

THANK GOODNESS THE CATS HAD left the room.

Tanner stroked the hair back from her face. Lili realized she clung to him as if she'd never let him go. After that momentous feeling, she didn't want to.

She wet her lips, then pulled back far enough to look at him. "I don't think anyone's ever done that to me before."

"Made you come?"

"No." She frowned, trying to find the words. "Made me forget where I was. And what we were talking about. And everything that was bothering me before…you did that."

"I've never made anyone feel like that."

Her calf was still up around his knee and she was balanced on one leg, his arms around her for support.

She put both feet flat on the floor, but hung on to him, though she did wriggle her bra and underwear back into place before she met his gaze again.

"I feel dizzy."

He chuckled. "So do I."

She drew in a deep breath. "I'm not sure how I feel about what we just did. I think I should be embarrassed or something because I was so out of control."

"You *think* you're embarrassed?"

"Well, actually, I'm not. But shouldn't I be?"

He caressed her throat. "I wouldn't like it if you were. I… That was important to me."

"But what were you saying before you did that? See, I can't remember. It was something about Erika." She rolled her eyes. "Oh, God, no. That would be awful. If we were talking about Erika and then *that* happened."

"It wasn't about Erika. I was saying that lying for you was justifiable."

"For me? I thought we lied to protect Erika."

"I lied to protect you. If you say Fluffy told you where the body was, Sheriff Gresswell will start investigating you."

"You mean he would have thought I killed the body?"

He laughed, not a wholehearted laugh, but more a sigh at the ridiculousness of what she'd said.

"I mean that I killed the man."

"I know what you meant. I don't know if he would have jumped to that immediate conclusion, but he would have asked a helluva lot more questions."

She looked at him, and they were so close, she couldn't see both eyes at once, so she switched from one blue orb to the other. Unlike earlier, his gaze was perfectly readable.

"I know the police won't believe me. You already told me that. But suspect me of...something? What?"

He didn't say anything.

"What do *you* suspect me of, Tanner?"

He sighed. "I really don't know."

"Yes, you do. You came over here to ask me something."

"Lili."

"You didn't come over here to make me come standing up."

He closed his eyes as if her bluntness was painful.

"I liked it, but you wanted to say something, and I stopped you, and now I think you'd better say whatever it was."

Even if she didn't want to hear it.

"Spit it out, Tanner," she whispered.

He sighed, then said it. "You're hiding something, and I want to know what it is. You got distant and thoughtful, and I know you well enough to say something was going on in that head of yours that you didn't tell me about."

She wriggled out of his arms, and her first thought was to deny it. But she couldn't. It was only a small thing, about Lady Dreadlock. But would Tanner think that was so small?

He reached out suddenly, putting his hands to the sides of her face, trapping her there. "Your face is like a pad of paper, and everything you think gets written on it. I just don't always know how to read it. So tell me."

She needed a minute to think about what to tell him. "Do you want a cup of tea?"

"No, thanks."

"Well, I need a cup of tea." She wanted the brighter lighting of the kitchen. If she was lucky, he wouldn't follow until she got herself under control.

Of course, Tanner followed her. Lili pulled out the plastic container where she stored her tea bags. Empty. She'd used the last one and hadn't refilled it.

She opened the cabinet over the counter, but even on her tiptoes, she couldn't quite reach the cellophane-wrapped box on the top shelf. Wanetta's cabinets were set a lot higher on the kitchen walls than the ones in Lili's ex-apartment.

Then Tanner was there, stretching up beside her to get the box, his body playing the length of hers. The contact sent a shiver racing through her. He was hard against her hip. He obviously still wanted her, and she oh, so certainly wanted him. At least her body did. It was her mind and heart she wasn't so sure about.

Sidestepping away, she fiddled with the cellophane.

"Lili." His voice was a puff of air stirring her hair, her female parts, her nipples once again aching little points.

She looked down. Even he would see them through the soft material of her blouse despite her bra. She wanted more of what he'd given her, wanted him inside her, all the way.

Yet she'd probably regret it when they were done, because there was one question she didn't know the answer to. She needed an answer before she let him in.

"I know you think the police won't believe me about Fluffy." She tossed her hair over her shoulder and tipped her head to look at him. "But do you believe me?"

He scanned her face, her forehead, her eyes, her

cheeks, then his gaze rested on her lips, and his focus on her mouth bore a carnal edge that stole her breath.

"I don't know," he said.

Neither his voice nor his words bore a trace of carnality, yet if she touched him, she knew he'd take her right on the kitchen floor. He'd given her a glorious release, but he hadn't had his. And he wanted it. She could scent his male need in the air, and like an aphrodisiac, it sent her blood rushing straight to her center.

It said something about his depth of feeling that he wanted her without being sure of her. That wasn't good enough for Lili. She had to know he believed in her before she committed herself to a relationship with him. He'd given her a sweet taste, but the full meal could cost her so much more.

"If you don't believe Fluffy told me, then how do you think I knew the body was out there?"

He touched her with the tip of his finger, tracing her lower lip. She wanted to suck him inside, take what he offered and worry about the consequences later. So she dug her nails in her palms, and the slight pain kept her from throwing herself at him.

He smoothed the back of his fingers across her cheek and into her hair, then cupped her nape, almost as if he needed to hold her still before he answered.

"Maybe you already knew the body was there." He shook his head when she opened her mouth. "You didn't have anything to do with how it got there, but you could have found it."

"But then why would I say Fluffy found it?"

"To provide concrete proof that you could talk to animals."

She took a moment to digest that before a phantom hand closed over her chest. The fact that he could even think it, let alone say it, squeezed the heart out of her. Somehow, it was so much worse than a simple matter of disbelief.

"So, not only am I a liar, I'm repulsive enough to use a cat, a little girl and an old man to further my own sick need for acceptance." She didn't jerk his hand away, didn't even pull from his oddly tender grip. "If I'm that bad, I don't know why you wouldn't think I killed him. To make sure there was a body to find."

He squeezed her neck, as if trying to remind her he had his hand on her and he wasn't letting go. "It isn't that bad."

"How could you even bear to touch me? Or kiss me? How could you make me come like that, as if you—" As if he cared.

He used that gentle hand to pull her closer, then tipped her head with a thumb under her chin. "Lili, it was an idle thought that ran through my mind. I was merely trying to find an explanation for the unexplainable."

He didn't get how bad it was. Worse than being Dirk's circus freak. Worse than Norton locking his puppy away from her.

He'd made love to her with his touch, if not his whole body, then he'd torn a hole right through her, but she didn't scream at him. She didn't cry.

"Tanner, do you think you could leave now? I'd like to enjoy my cup of tea alone and properly digest what you've said."

She'd save the crying for later, when she figured out whether she'd recover or not.

"THAT WAS FAST." ROSCOE PULLED out beers for the boys.

Tanner was next door visiting Lili—hohoho, that was a boon Roscoe hadn't expected—and Erika was upstairs watching TV. Actually, she was trying to calm Fluffy down once again. That cat had the most nervous constitution, even before his night up in the tree. Why, as soon as he'd heard Chester's car in the drive, he'd bolted. He was getting downright paranoid over people in the house.

However, with Tanner and Erika out of sight, Roscoe smelled an advantage coming his way.

"I heard it on the police scanner," Linwood said as he scraped a chair along the linoleum and sat. "So, I called up Chester and we grabbed Hiram, too." In his haste, he'd forgotten to put on his medals. He kept them in a wooden box on the top shelf of his closet. He claimed they shouldn't be exposed to the light any longer than necessary, though he usually found it essential to wear them everywhere he went.

"Linwood wants to know the whole story," Hiram groused. "He's an old busybody. You'd think the man had female genes."

"Take that back, Hiram." Linwood shook his fist. "You were the one who suggested we rush right over here."

Roscoe handed round the beers, then pulled out the only empty chair at the kitchen table, set his foot on it and leaned on his knee.

"So you want the scoop. What's it worth to ya?" He liked being the center of attention. More, he liked having the upper hand. Especially with Hiram, who usually had the upper hand on all of them.

"You're dying to tell us, you old faker." Chester wiped a speck of foam from his chin.

So he was—faking it, that was. He was dying to tell all, because a plan had blossomed the moment he'd heard that old Lincoln crunch the gravel in the drive. Chester and Linwood were the biggest gossips in town. And they loved their morning gabfests down at the Coffee Stain.

"Well, it started with Lili."

"Who's Lili?" Chester asked.

Roscoe resisted rolling his eyes. "You met her last night, the one that looked like Deanna Durbin."

"Oh yeah. She was a pretty little thing."

"And she talks to animals."

Hiram harrumphed. He was a good harrumpher. "Get on with the story."

And Roscoe began to explain.

By morning, everyone in Benton would hear that Lili had known about the body before it had been found. Tanner would be put to the test. The sheriff would start asking questions about Lili, and Roscoe was sure Tanner wouldn't simply throw her to the wolves. He'd have to protect her. Not that Lili would really need protection. After all, she was innocent. Gresswell would figure that out almost the minute he started talking to her.

It was a devious plan. But his son needed a lot of help figuring out that Lili was the perfect woman for him. And the perfect mother for Erika.

CHESTER PAWSON'S LINCOLN SAT in the driveway behind Tanner's sedan. If he hadn't been blocked in, he was sure he'd have climbed behind the wheel and taken off into the night so he could get his head screwed on straight.

She didn't cry. She didn't yell. Her very lack of reaction showed how badly he'd hurt her. She'd kicked him out with only two sentences. The Lili he knew would have taken at least five.

He should have lied. Sometimes there was an excellent reason to lie. When your honest thoughts would hurt. Or maim. He'd just maimed Lili. In his search to justify why he simply couldn't believe in her, he'd maimed her.

Tanner pushed back through the hedge. He couldn't leave it that way. Not after she'd gone off in his arms and blown the top off his world. He knocked on her back door. Both the kitchen and the porch light went out in response. He opened the screen door and tried the knob. It was locked.

"Lili. Open up. We need to talk about this. I'm sorry." Dammit, he shouldn't have left in the first place.

Something thumped the porch and a large object slinked across the wood slats and stopped right at his feet. Einstein the cat. Tanner sidestepped to let it by. Only it didn't crawl off the other side of the porch and into the night. It sat. And looked at him. The moonlight revealed wide green eyes, a hint of long canines, gray tail twitching back and forth, back and forth.

He could swear it was talking.

You are scum.

Tanner couldn't agree more.

He needed to talk to Lili, to explain. He went around front. The cat followed, jumped up on the porch railing and stared. It was unnerving. Tanner tried that door, too. Also locked. Then he stepped back off the porch and looked up at the second floor. The hall light went out, then the bedroom light, or at least what he assumed was her bedroom, and the house lay in darkness. Silent as a tomb.

Until the cat jumped down from the railing with a thump.

"I didn't think what I said was that bad."

Einstein blinked, opened its mouth wide, its teeth pointy and sharp, and yawned. Then it flopped onto a back haunch, raised a hind leg in the air and starting licking itself.

There was a definite message in that. *Kiss my ass, bud.*

The best he could do was tell Lili he was sorry. He was a dolt for ever voicing that thought aloud.

The problem was he still believed he'd found a damn good explanation for how she'd known the body was out in the woods.

CHAPTER ELEVEN

LILI DIDN'T CRY AFTER TANNER left last night. Locking her doors against him and shutting out all the lights had been liberating, giving her back a measure of equilibrium. But it didn't provide any answers as to why his words hurt *this* badly. She was used to inspiring a whole host of reactions to her ability, some of them not very nice, but she'd always been able to put the unpleasant experiences behind her and move on. Why couldn't she do that with Tanner?

Over tuna-fish sandwiches and a soda, he'd offered her the world. He'd asked for her help with Erika. He'd trusted her with *the* most important person in his life. Sure, he'd gotten squirrelly again, but that was understandable. Lili had gotten squirrelly in the field, and it had taken *hours* to recover.

But she'd thought they were past that. The way he'd touched her, he had to be past that. But it didn't mean a thing to him.

She'd been thought of as a crackpot, whacked-out weirdo before, but never a devious, lowlife user.

She had to stop thinking about it.

This morning she had more important things to do than dwell on Tanner's opinion of her. Which was why, at ten minutes after eight, Lili loaded Einstein into the front basket of her bike and took off for town. In deference to the cool spring air, she'd worn a heavy fleece sweatshirt, but her legs were bare from the tops of her tennis shoes to the bottom of her capri pants. It really was easier riding her bike in pants rather than a skirt. She did a good job of tucking it away from the bike chain, but sometimes... She had ruined a couple of skirts.

As Lili pedaled down the hill, Einstein put her head into the wind like the hood ornament on a car or the carving on the prow of a Viking ship. They were off to find Lady Dreadlock, and Einstein was going to do some cat-to-human interpreting. Lili was glad she hadn't told Tanner about the woman last night. She'd figure out Lady D. on her own. If she learned something the police needed to know, she'd tell them. She didn't need Tanner's permission to do what she knew was right.

And Tanner was *not* going to stop her.

Like a simmering pot, Lili felt her own anger just below the surface. It wasn't like her. She hated it. Anger was a useless emotion. Tanner made her feel a lot of things she wasn't used to feeling. That gave him way too much power.

With the light green at the bottom of the hill, Lili took the corner too quickly and the bike wobbled. Einstein hunkered down and sent an unmentionable image.

At only a little after eight on a Sunday morning, minimal traffic cluttered the highway winding through the redwoods. The bike lanes were wide, the speed limit was only thirty-five, and there was a separate bike path to cross the twin bridges before you got into Benton.

Early morning joggers ran the track at the high school, and the church parking lot was filling up for the half-past eight service. On Sundays, the Coffee Stain opened at 6:30 instead of the usual weekday 5:00 a.m. start, and the aroma of fresh, rich, dark, yummy coffee wafted through the open doors as Lili rode past.

Work first, then she could reward herself with a mocha. She'd stuffed a few bills in her pocket.

The parking spaces along the front were filled; a dog was leashed to a tree and a man exited carrying a holder of cups, but Lady Dreadlock was not haunting the coffeehouse sidewalk. One spot down, a million more to go.

Lili pedaled round the cars in front of the Copper Penny diner, the only other place open at this time of the morning. After that, the street was empty. She made her way down to the end of town, past the sheriff's department, then back along some side streets. She hooked a right at the intersection where the sidewalk ended and rode at the edge of the gravel beneath the trees that hung over the street like an arbor. The lots along Maple Street were smaller than in the hills where Lili now lived, and most had grass, tended gardens, large, shady oaks and white picket fences. She passed her old house where she'd had a flat on the top floor. Someone had put out a planter of geraniums. A small pang wedged up under her breast. She hadn't expected to see a change in only one week.

But she had Wanetta's house. A home that was hers.

The road dead-ended into a walking entrance to the county park. Lili stopped the bike before it, in front of the halfway house, an old Victorian renovated a few years ago. She'd saved it for last because, well, walking up the front steps and knocking on the door felt the most confrontational. White rattan chairs sat haphazardly on the front porch, though no one was sitting outside right now. The house was dark blue with white trim, three dormer windows perched along the roofline, but not even a curtain fluttered with a sign of life.

Einstein raised her head, sniffed, then jumped from the basket, landed gracefully and sauntered toward the park entrance.

"We are not looking for gophers now. I need to see if she's in the house." Einstein twitched her whiskers, then headed into the park.

"You'd better be smelling her," Lili muttered, but it was also a relief not to have to go pounding on the front door.

She followed Einstein, wheeling her bike through the gate. She did not listen to Tanner's voice in her head saying she was stupid. Under the trees, the earth smelled…earthier. Wildflowers were starting to bloom, yellow, white, blue, a few orange poppies were scattered about, and the new ferns were a lush green. Lili had the urge to pick some for her next tinkering project.

Ignore it, babe. We're on a mission.

Einstein didn't have to tell her. This was *her* mission, after all. Suddenly Tanner's words hit her again. Was she out here because she *did* need to prove something to him?

No, she was on a humanitarian effort. To save Lady Dreadlock from herself. Or the police? Or…aw, hell, why couldn't she stop thinking about Tanner? About the sweetness of his kiss, his spicy male scent, the rough texture of his fingers…and the slam of what he really thought of her.

She walked the bike, trailing Einstein's straight-up

tail along the narrow path. The grasses snicked over her bare calves and left burrs in the hem of her capris.

Then Einstein veered to the right, stopped next to the huge trunk of a mighty oak, swished her tail and sat.

She's here. An image of dreadlocks whispered through Lili's mind.

What's she doing? Actually, she imaged a question mark, but Einstein was excellent in extrapolating.

Come and find out.

Said the spider to the fly. Lili pushed down her kickstand, left the bike behind and leaned around the oak by Einstein.

Lady Dreadlock sat cross-legged on the ground, her hands resting palm up on her knees, her fingers lightly touching. And oh, Lord, she was naked. At least she wasn't facing them. A pile of clothing lay on the forest floor beside her. A big pile. Probably everything she owned.

I can't talk to her naked.

You're not naked.

Not me. Her. Lili felt a blush of heat rise to her face.

In case you haven't noticed, I'm naked. What's wrong with being naked? As I recall, you were bareassed last night.

Oh. Oh. That was a low blow. She'd never have expected it from her cat. Einstein's whiskers twitched. Then she padded into the small clearing. Lili looked around to make sure there wasn't any poison oak. That poor woman, if there was. The ground was littered with leaves and dead ferns, and a small votive candle burned on a cracked saucer.

Why, Lady D. was meditating. Lili could now hear

her soft, musical hum. A sweet sound that seemed almost a part of the breeze passing over her, it wasn't a tune so much as a series of tones that melded with the forest around her and the earth beneath her. It touched something deep inside Lili and brought an immediate mistiness to her eyes.

Lady D. was brown all over—not that Lili looked *all* over—and thin, so thin. Her arms were like sticks, and her collarbones stark against her leathery flesh. It wasn't so much starvation of the body as starvation of the soul.

The woman was gaunt with self-loathing. Lili couldn't say how she knew it. It didn't come from Einstein. It was as if the woman's aura actually spoke to Lili and in the swirling mass of purple darkness surrounding Lady Dreadlock eddied a profound sadness, a devastating fear. It was almost choking.

Einstein lay down and stretched her forelegs out like a sphinx. Her tail, a sticker in the tip, twitched, then settled. *Ask her about the puppy.*

What puppy?

Einstein gave her the dunce cap.

Lili sat cross-legged on the ground at the base of her own oak and studied the woman's profile.

"I'm sorry about the puppy," she said, using a soft voice in keeping with the sanctity of the forest.

"I knew what you were," Lady D. said.

Lili tilted her head. *I know what you are.* That was what the woman had always started with. But this time her tense was past, and it changed everything. She was talking about a specific event.

Lili said what felt natural. "I didn't mean to hurt the puppy."

"God was watching you."

Again, that odd past tense. Lady Dreadlock had seen her with a puppy. Yes, Lili remembered the first time the woman had confronted her. Lili had been talking to a puppy outside the Stain. The poor little thing couldn't understand why he'd been tied to a tree as if he were unloved and unwanted.

"You knew what I was doing, didn't you?" Lili kept speaking with the same, soft tone.

"God thought you were bad."

"For talking to the puppy?"

Lady Dreadlock turned her deep, soulful brown eyes on Lili, and for the first time, Lili didn't see the censure she'd always believed was there.

"Don't let God punish you."

There was an unspoken statement, but Lili heard it, knew in her heart what the rest of it was.

Don't let God punish you the way He's punished me. That was what Lady D. meant.

"God didn't punish you because you can talk to animals. That's God's blessing. Einstein, tell her."

Lady D. tipped her head and looked at Einstein. Then she closed her eyes, and her head bobbed slightly, rhythmically. It was the oddest feeling. Lili couldn't interpret a thing, and she suddenly realized this was how it must look to others when she talked to animals. Not Einstein, because they'd been together so long and understood so quickly. But other animals, the ones Lili had to concentrate with, turning inward, blanking out everyone around her. And coming off looking as if she were crazy.

She suddenly saw what all three of them would

look like to the outside world beyond this small clearing surrounded by trees and ferns and wildflowers. How she sounded to Tanner with all her talk about animals and Bigfoot.

Einstein slanted her eyes at Lili. *She doesn't believe us.*

Of course she didn't. If Lady Dreadlock had been talking to animals as long as Lili had, whatever she'd come to believe about herself was ingrained.

Lili didn't know how to help her. "You're not bad, and God's not mad."

Einstein made a noise at her very poor rhyme. Lili admitted it sounded ridiculous, but it had slipped out.

Lady D. merely blinked in the same fashion as Einstein.

"Okay. So, that's not going to work. Maybe you should tell me your name so I can stop calling you Lady Dreadlock."

It was like talking to a blank wall. Lady D. was only capable of a variation on the theme of being bad and God punishing her.

Maybe Lili could talk to her social worker. She was pretty sure they had social workers at the halfway house.

Ha! She could hear herself explaining that the reason the woman seemed as if she was off her rocker was that she couldn't come to grips with her ability to talk to animals. Then they'd be putting Lili herself into the halfway house.

All right, this would take some serious consideration. Rome wasn't built in a day, and mental illness wasn't cured with a half hour feel-good talk in a forest.

Right now, there was another immediate issue.

"Did you see something bad happen in the meadow?"

The blank wall stared back.

"Send her an image, Einstein."

The two of them did that weird communication thing again. And it was bizarre, sort of voyeuristic. Lili wished Lady Dreadlock had her clothes on, because being naked added to the weirdness.

She did see Fluffy, as an emasculated feline. Really, Einstein needed to get over this little problem she had with Fluffy.

"Was it on the night in question?" She sounded like a lawyer.

Can't quite tell.

Lili pressed her lips together. Lady Dreadlock had seen Fluffy, and since Fluffy had stuck by the house for the last three days, the meeting had to have taken place sometime while he'd been out *that* night. Or coming back in the morning.

"Did you see it?" she whispered to the woman. "Do you know what happened? Do you know who did it?"

Lady D. shivered, closed her eyes, then leaned forward and blew out the candle.

Lili looked at Einstein. Einstein stared back.

Lady Dreadlock knew something. As much as Lili hated causing the woman problems, let alone the ramifications to the halfway house, she had to tell the police.

"HOW'RE YOU DOING THIS MORNING, kiddo?"

Erika's voice came from somewhere amid the jumble of pillows and the thick comforter.

Tanner sat on the edge of the bed and pulled back the lavender bedclothes so he could see her. Instead, Fluffy gave him a gloomy gaze. Tanner bit back his immediate retort. Erika wasn't supposed to have the cat *in* the bed, but yesterday had been an unusual day, to say the least, and his daughter obviously needed the cat's comfort as much as it needed hers.

"Where are you under there?" Tanner poked around.

The comforter flapped back to reveal his daughter's blond head and a set of dark circles under her eyes that made her look like a zombie. Her gaze was as gloomy as Fluffy's.

"You okay, sweetheart? You slept pretty late." Erika was usually the first one up on a Sunday morning, but when the downstairs grandfather clock had struck eight, Tanner had felt compelled to come looking for her.

"It took a while to calm Fluffy down last night." She scratched the cat's head. "He's better now, though."

Yeah, because it'd been treated like a king instead of a cat. "I know you're worried about Fluffy."

"I'm worried about Lili, too."

"Lili?"

"I heard you and Grandpa talking last night. Do you think the police will believe she had something to do with the murder?"

Damn. His little girl didn't miss much, which was why he should have kept his mouth shut with her in the house. No wonder she'd been virtually silent at dinner. He'd tried reassuring her last night when he'd tucked her in, but he hadn't realized the bent of her thoughts.

He'd been thinking about other things, dammit. Lili.

With that serious gaze, his daughter seemed so adult. Lili was right. Erika was on the cusp of womanhood, and he hadn't paid attention to it. He didn't want her to grow up. He didn't want her to turn thirteen. At twelve, she was still a child. With the teenage years, all hell broke loose, and she wouldn't be his little girl anymore.

What was he supposed to say when she—gulp—started. He couldn't even say the real word for it, so how was he supposed to talk to her about it?

He'd have to get some feminine influence in her life, as Lili had suggested. He wasn't sure anymore if *Lili* was the right influence. Too much had happened since he'd asked for Lili's help yesterday. Maybe he should ask someone from the Big Sisters organization, someone older and wiser who couldn't talk to Fluffy.

"You do think the police will suspect her, don't you, Dad?"

"What do you think, Erika? What will the police say?"

She rolled and gathered Fluffy close. The cat stuck its front legs out, stretched, then sprawled on the bed. "Well, on TV, the police always look for ulterior motives," she said over the cat's immense belly.

"This isn't TV."

"But *you* think she has ulterior motives."

He'd brought this on himself. "Remember what I told you yesterday before Lili and I went out? You have to decide for yourself. I can't tell you what to think about Lili. And I don't know what the police will say." He folded Erika's hand into his. "I do know I don't want to see her hurt, and that's part of why I didn't say anything." He'd been harsh yesterday, throwing edicts at his daughter. Erika was getting to the point where she needed explanations, especially since he'd introduced her to lying.

"Well, she sort of comes off as an airhead when you

first meet her. But then she grows on you. Now, I really think Lili's a good person. And when there's a little bit of evidence *for* someone and a little bit of evidence *against* them, you have to go with that feeling in your tummy and believe in them."

His daughter was a better person than he was. If he'd been thinking like Erika, he never would have crushed Lili last night. Maybe he wouldn't even have had the thought in the first place.

"I'm proud of you for making up your own mind based on such a good rationale." Even if it did involve gut instinct. Sometimes that *could* be the most important sense. Then again, sometimes not.

"Well," Erika said, "that's why we should do everything we can to help her."

"We will, sweetie."

"So I think I should tell you that Grandpa told Chester and Linwood and Hiram that Lili knew about the body before you found it."

He jumped off the bed as if a bomb had exploded under him. "What?"

"So the police are going to know about that soon, too."

The next body found out in the woods was going to be Roscoe's. Because Tanner was going to kill the old man.

"WHERE WAS YOUR HEAD, ROSCOE?"

Roscoe waved his spatula, and a few drops of waffle batter spattered on the floor. He decided he'd clean it up later. "They won't say anything. I told them to keep it on the Q.T."

"They do not know how to be quiet."

"Don't you like them?"

"They're not a bad bunch, but Chester and Linwood are like gossiping old ladies, usually harmless, but this time…" Giving Roscoe a sharp look, Tanner let the words trail off.

True, true. Hiram wasn't so bad, mostly because his position up at the college required a certain amount of decorum, but Chester and Linwood…ah yes, they'd do Roscoe's dirty work.

"You worry too much, Tanner. You're going to give yourself a heart attack. I'm making waffles. Do you want me to whip up some cream?"

"And waffles with whipped cream *won't* give me a heart attack?" Tanner turned a circle in the middle of the kitchen floor, dragging a hand down his freshly shaven face. "Roscoe, what did we talk about yesterday? Protecting Lili, remember?"

Heeheehee. Perfect, perfect. Tanner was reacting just as Roscoe wanted him to. "She'll be fine. It's not as if she did anything wrong, so what's the big deal? The police aren't going to hustle her off to jail and shine bright lights in her face until she confesses all under duress."

"I can't believe I'm having to say this to you. Even Erika has more sense." Tanner threw his hands up in the air and puffed out a disgusted breath. "I'm going over to warn Lili. While I'm gone, I want you to call your buddies and tell them if they open their mouths, they'll have to deal with me."

Roscoe mopped up the batter he'd spilled. "Will do. Why don't you invite Lili for waffles, too?"

Tanner gave him a look and slammed through the screen door.

Perfect. Something had gone on last night while Tanner had been over at dear Lili's, if that shell-shocked look he'd returned with meant anything. Something more would go on this morning.

He'd have to make sure that little smartie-pants upstairs got with the program. She might have spoiled the whole thing with her big mouth. Roscoe had had it in mind that Tanner would hear about it down in town. He smiled. *All's well that ends well.* He was sure Erika would fall right in with his plan.

After all, she'd gobbled up that book Roscoe happened to see hidden behind the couch. If she played her cards right, the name of the book would soon be *Erika's New Mom.*

Now, he had to make sure Tanner invited Lili along on their excursion down to the Boardwalk the next night for Erika's spring break from school, which started tomorrow.

If Tanner didn't invite her, Roscoe would issue the invitation himself.

SO SHE'D GO TO THE POLICE, but first Lili needed mocha fortification at the Coffee Stain. She coasted along the sidewalk, then skimmed to a stop by the front window, swung off the bike and flipped down her kickstand.

She bent close to Einstein. "I'll be right back. Do not talk to any strangers."

What about people I know?

"Don't get smart with me." Then she scratched behind Einstein's ears and kissed the tip of her nose.

A hush fell as she passed through the open door. It

was darn hard for ten people to fall silent all at once, and that wasn't counting Manny and the girls behind the counter. Lili got a bad feeling.

Seated at a table for two in the back against the wall, she recognized Chester and Linwood from Roscoe's the other night. Hey, maybe this was an opportunity to offer them Cy and Rita. After her mocha was in her hands, of course. Lili smiled and waved. They stared with big, wide eyes.

The whispering at the other tables started. A woman punched in numbers on her cell, never taking her eyes off Lili. So how did she get the number correct? Whatever. Lili shook her head. She knew hardly any of these people by name, but most of the faces were familiar. In a short while, the day trippers from over the hill would be arriving and the place would be hopping, but for now, most were locals.

Lili squeezed between the big ficus and the couple waiting at the drip coffee counter, the rich scent of coffee heady and mouthwatering. But the middle-aged couple—the one couple she didn't recognize—stared.

She sidled past the Danish counter and got in line behind a large man she knew was a contractor. She'd seen his truck around. There were two other customers ahead of him, a man and a teenage girl with a nose ring.

Manny's voice boomed out. "We can't let our celebrity wait in line, and honey bunch, the mocha is on the house today. I'm even going to make it a triple shot." Manny waved her forward and the three in line ahead of her backed up against the refrigerated drink unit to give her plenty of room. As if she were a rock star. Or a suspected serial killer.

"Get this little lady's triple shot white mocha foaming, sweetie pie."

"Sweetie pie" had a dolphin tattoo above her butt cheek and her hip huggers were low enough to show it. Lili didn't have a clue what her real name was.

"So, honey bunch, tell me why you were holding out on me."

Lili felt her eyes go as wide as Chester and Linwood's had been. *Please, don't let it be.* She was hoping and praying it wasn't so. "Holding out on what?"

"Don't give me that crap. You're going to be on *Oprah.*" He circled his hand in the air. "Better yet, you'll have your own show. You'll be like those ghostbuster guys where people call 'em up from all over the country and pay them the big bucks to solve their ghost problems. They drive some cool vans, too."

She was overheating in the heavy fleece she'd worn against the morning chill. "Manny, I don't know what you're talking about." Oh, but she did. Tanner was going to annihilate her.

"Don't play possum, honey bunch. You found that body out back a' Buddy Welch's place after a cat told you it was there." He raised his hands as if he were standing in a pulpit instead of behind a cash register in the Stain. "Isn't that the damnedest thing, folks? A cat told her there'd been a murder, and she went right out and found the body. And the murderer, too."

Manny was teasing, laying it on so thick it was worse than giving Einstein peanut butter. But Lili felt breath on the back of her neck. The large contractor. She hugged closer to the register. Her temples started to throb. The couple at the drip counter grabbed their cups before the coffee had even finished dripping, snapped on their lids and rushed out the door backward as if they were afraid to take their eyes off Lili.

"Now the cops," Manny went on, "have got Buddy Welch in their sights. He's a menace. Bet it was some trespasser, and he blew the guy's head off. You're a hero, honey bunch."

Oh, oh, it was worse than she thought. "He wasn't shot."

Manny wasn't listening to anyone but himself, and his voice got louder as the espresso machine built up its head of steam. "I'm sure they'll be arresting him right after the sheriff gets back from church." He leaned over the counter and chucked her under the chin. "I'll never doubt you again. The next time you tell me a cockroach talked to you in my place, I'm damn well gonna get out the bug spray."

"I was joking about the cockroach." But how did Manny know about the body? About Buddy? About any of it? Lili glanced at her watch. It wasn't quite nine-thirty yet. Then she turned slowly to the pocket of tables along the wall, to one suspiciously empty table. Chester and Linwood were gone. But they were Roscoe's friends. And Roscoe knew...

Tanner was going to annihilate her *and* Roscoe.

Something bumped Lili's bare leg between the top of her socks and the bottom of her capris. A furry cat head. Einstein smiled up at her. Oh yeah, cats could smile, bared teeth and all. The little rat was having fun watching her predicament.

"I thought I told you to stay in the basket."

"See. She's doing it, folks, right before your very eyes."

I suggest you get out front. Pronto. Lili saw herself being catapulted out the front door.

She tapped the counter, then backed away. "You know, Manny, I'd better skip the triple shot. Too much caffeine. Not to mention all that chocolate."

When she turned, she saw Tanner outside the front window. Standing by her bike. Staring right at her. That was not a happy-camper look on his face. Well, she wasn't going to let him intimidate her.

But she did need fortification.

"On second thought, Manny, could you make that a quadruple shot?"

CHAPTER TWELVE

LILI WORE A THICK SWEATER yet her calves were bare, and she wrapped her hands around her huge cup of coffee for warmth. Or as if it were a ward against Tanner's wrath.

Was he truly such an ogre? Yeah, actually he was. At least he had been to her.

It wasn't cold, but the spring chill wouldn't completely wear off until noon. Keeping her eyes on him, Lili blew through the hole in her coffee lid, then sipped.

"Fancy meeting you here," she said.

"No accident. I saw the cat."

Einstein blinked its green eyes and crawled between the wall and Lili's front tire, the spokes caging her in, or protecting her against the coming fireworks. The cat had jumped from the bike's basket, hackles raised, before Tanner had gotten out of his car.

Right after his talk with Roscoe, he'd gone over to Lili's. The doors were locked, and when he'd seen her bike missing from the front porch, he'd been consumed by an overpowering anger. First, that she could be so stupid as to leave her house when there was a murderer loose who, because of Roscoe's idiocy, undoubtedly knew or would know that Lili had seen him, even if through a cat's eyes. Okay, she didn't know what Roscoe had done, but she did know there was a murderer loose. Second, that he himself could get so worked up about something that was nothing because who in their right mind—if a killer could be in his right mind—would worry about what Fluffy saw anyway, so honestly, what was the danger? And third, that he couldn't stop thinking about her, worrying about her, wanting her, regretting what he'd said last night and regretting that he hadn't made love to her when he'd had the chance.

He was over the anger now, after half an hour of driving around looking for her.

Lili flicked her braid forward over her shoulder and played with the end. It did something odd to his insides, the brush of her hair on her cheek, back and forth, back and forth. It was mesmerizing. Lili constantly had that effect on him.

"I think you should know," she said.

Tanner cut her off. "I already know."

"How?"

"Roscoe. And a bit of deductive reasoning."

"But do you know the same thing I think you know?" In the midst of crisis, she wrenched a laugh from him.

She stared at him with those guileless lilac eyes. "I wasn't trying to be funny."

"I know. Let's walk down the street a bit." Right now they were framed in the front window of the Coffee Stain as if they were contestants on the latest reality show.

She stopped in front of the currently closed Mane Man barbershop next door. "This is far enough."

Einstein inched from the front tire to the back tire and

kept up the glare. That cat really didn't like him. Or it loved Lili a helluva lot. Or both.

Tanner played her word game. "So, tell me what you think I know."

She tipped her head slightly as if she appreciated his effort. "Everyone at the Stain knows about Fluffy and me."

"You're right, I knew that."

"But did you know the police know, too? At least that's what Manny says."

Tanner tried not to react. He certainly didn't want to get mad, but how the hell could news have traveled so fast? Oh yeah, Chester and Linwood and half an hour at the Coffee Stain on a Sunday morning. It made perfect sense.

Lili blinked at him. "You didn't get mad."

"I'm turning over a new leaf."

She beamed at him. Beamed, no less, like a hundred-watt bulb right in the eyes. "That's wonderful."

It was as if last night hadn't happened, as if he hadn't trashed her feelings nor taken her to those exquisite heights. The former was good, the latter untenable. He didn't want her to even remember what he'd said, but he sure as hell wanted her to have *some* emotion about what they'd done.

"Okay. Here's the thing."

She was irrepressible, undaunted, unquenchable. And irresistible. He expanded his chest with a deep breath, then let it out long and slow.

"Sorry. I forgot I wasn't supposed to use that expression."

"Spit it out, Lili." Damn, she made him want so much

more. In the midst of murder and mayhem right in his own backyard, Lili made him *want*.

"I should have told you yesterday that I saw Lady Dreadlock in the meadow the day before. But I needed time to think about whether I should say anything to anyone at all, not just you. Then this morning, Einstein and I talked to her, and now I know I need to say something."

He pulled her to him and kissed her full on the lips. Hard.

"Why'd you do that?" she asked when he let her go, her gaze wide, her eyes glassy.

"Because if I didn't, I would have had to yell at you. And I don't feel like yelling even though I am pissed." It was a relative term. He was torn between shaking some sense into her and kissing her until she couldn't think straight. Or he couldn't think straight. "Why the hell didn't you say that yesterday?"

He knew the answer with gut-clenching clarity. Deep down, Lili didn't trust him, not to believe in her, not to protect her and not to hurt her.

They'd have to talk about what he'd said last night. Only not now in the middle of the sidewalk outside Mane Man. Church was out, and the street was starting to fill up with cars and the sidewalks with people, strollers, bikes and skateboards.

"Scratch that question. I don't care why at this point. Who is Lady Dreadlock?"

When she finished telling him, he was more confused than before she'd started explaining. Lili did that to a man, turned his thought processes inside out and upside down.

"So, let me paraphrase. This crazy woman—"

"She's not really crazy—"

He held up his hand. She shut her mouth. "This crazy woman has been hassling you for months, but you haven't reported her to the police. Then you saw her in the woods the evening you went *alone* to look for the body. Now she's told you that she talks to animals, and she saw Fluffy the morning after the supposed night that my cat saw a murder. Have I got that right?"

"Well, it's right except the part about Lady D. telling me. She told Einstein, and Einstein told me."

He wanted to bang his head against the concrete wall next to Mane Man's front window. If he'd thought he was having trouble with the one thing—Fluffy telling Lili about a murder—then he was facing a catastrophe with the rest of what she'd said.

He would, however, persevere. "So that's all of it?"

She chewed her bottom lip. "Um, yeah, I think that's it."

"You're not forgetting to tell me anything on purpose?"

"Definitely not. That's everything. But you're talking to me as if I'm a child."

"You're right. I'm sorry. That was unconscionable."

"And I don't think you mean that."

"Lili."

"But we can talk about that later."

They'd talk about a few things of his choosing, as well. "All right. Then let's get over to the sheriff's department."

She looked at him over the rim of her coffee lid.

He was forced to ask. "What?"

"Aren't you going to yell or freak out or something?"

"No."

"Why not? Maybe I'm making up the thing about Lady Dreadlock to get more attention."

So. She hadn't gotten over his miscalculation of the prior evening. He wouldn't have believed her to be so adept at hiding her feelings.

"Lili, about last night—"

She put a hand over one ear and her coffee cup to the other. "I don't want to hear it. I'm so over last night. Let's talk to the sheriff."

She might be over it, but Tanner knew he wasn't. Not by a long shot.

SHERIFF GRESSWELL'S DESK was the size of a postage stamp and his office was, comparatively speaking, a postcard instead of an eight-and-a-half-by-eleven envelope. If the sheriff had been taller than five-ten and bigger than one-hundred-sixty pounds, he probably wouldn't fit through the door. But then the sheriff's department was housed in a one-story office building with a tax firm on one side and a holistic healing center on the other. They didn't have a jail—they had to take criminals down to the municipal building—and when they called out the SWAT team, the members mobilized in the parking lot. It didn't accommodate much more than the SWAT van itself. When the nondenominational Bible school across the highway had complained, the city council had asked the SWAT to mobilize outside the high school gym, but that had proven distracting when school was in session so they were back to using the parking lot, and the church just had to suffer.

Thank God they weren't mobilizing today.

Sheriff Gresswell scratched a hand through his short but explosively curly gray hair. Lili thought she heard a few strands snap. He still wore his Sunday best.

He spoke to Tanner. "I was going to drop by your place today. To clear up any loose ends."

Lili felt those loose ends tightening around her neck like a noose. Why hadn't Tanner lost his cool with her? She'd have felt better. He'd kissed her instead, and she didn't know what that meant. She would have been more comfortable tackling Sheriff Gresswell on her own, but there was no way Tanner would let her get away with that. They'd stashed her bike in the back room of the flower shop—which was closed on Sunday—rather than stuffing it in his trunk, and left Einstein in the shop's front window surveying the street from beneath the philodendron leaves.

Tanner didn't think bringing a cat along was going to help Lili's case.

"Do you have any idea yet who he was?" Tanner asked.

"Not yet. All the medical examiner can tell us is that he was a Caucasian male in his early twenties. We took his prints." He glanced at Lili. "What there was of them, at any rate."

Oh. Oh. She didn't want to think what *wasn't* there.

Turning back to Tanner, the sheriff said, "We're running them through the system, but so far no matches."

Then he smiled at Lili. A nice smile, with nice white teeth and plenty of crinkles at his eyes. He had the lined, weathered face of a man who spent time outdoors, but he didn't have the worn crags she would have expected in someone who spent his days and nights dealing with teenagers playing with drugs, spouses beating on their loved ones and bodies that had lain out in the elements long enough to attract the vultures.

Maybe he had a loving wife who soothed those lines

and crags away. Or maybe he needed a cat. Bash would be perfect for him. After a hard day battling criminals, he'd be glad to come home to a cat who only wanted to love and be loved. Now, however, wasn't the time to bring Bash up.

"Speaking of loose ends, Sheriff." Lili tapped her finger on the arm of her chair. Though they'd gotten past the loose-end thing, it still felt like a good jumping off point. "There was something I forgot when I talked to your deputies yesterday." That wasn't a lie. She hadn't remembered Lady Dreadlock being in the field until she and Tanner had been on their way back home.

Tanner shifted in his chair, putting his elbow on the armrest close enough for his body heat to reach out to her. It was comforting. Sheriff Gresswell raised a bushy gray eyebrow.

Lili wanted a fortifying sip of coffee, but instead she plunged on. "When I was out walking in the woods Friday night, I saw someone. I don't know her name, but I'm sure she lives down in the halfway house at the end of Maple Street, and she was in the field where we found the—" she gulped "—well, you know, and she might have seen something that could be helpful to you."

The sheriff's expression seemed a little wiped clean. No smile, no frown. He didn't even roll his eyes at her. "What does this *someone* look like?"

Translation: "I believe in *someone* like I believe in Bigfoot and little green men."

Still, Lili answered his question. "She's got a big bunch of dreadlocks." She waved her hands around her head, as if that would help the sheriff see. "You know, where they twist up their hair in long tails." Rat's tails,